"I've been tracking your movements with GPS. There are devices in the truck and in your wallet."

Skylar looked down at her purse.

Finished loading the truck, she closed the tailgate and faced him. "What else have you done?"

"Not as much as I'd like to." Although he hadn't meant the double entendre, his eyes raked down the front of her blouse.

When he returned his gaze to hers, he caught her finishing her own appreciative observation. He grinned.

"What I meant is I'd rather be near you 24/7 to protect you. That attack proves how vulnerable you are," Julien said.

"I know what you meant." Her soft smile remained as she seemed to consider something else. "I don't let men I just met move in with me."

"I wouldn't be moving in. I'd be a houseguest for a while. Separate bedrooms."

Her smile slowly eased away, but a flirtatious light glinted in her eyes. "Why don't we start with dinner? Then I'll decide."

"Dinner it is." He'd be sure to pack a bag, too.

Dear Reader,

I hope you are enjoying the Chelseys as much as I enjoy writing their stories! I introduced Cal in *Cold Case Manhunt*, and now I offer you his sister Skylar's story. Danger abounds after she witnesses a man trying to bury a body. Lucky for her, Cal has a friend and coworker in Julien Lacroix. Julien has his hands full protecting Skylar, and neither can resist their attraction. That's what makes these stories so rewarding.

Look ahead for stories about the Chelseys' neighbor and one about Cal and Skylar's brother, Corbin. I can't wait!

Jennifer Morey

HER P.I.
PROTECTOR

Jennifer Morey

HARLEQUIN
ROMANTIC
SUSPENSE

HARLEQUIN®
ROMANTIC SUSPENSE™

Recycling programs
for this product may
not exist in your area.

ISBN-13: 978-1-335-62671-4

Her P.I. Protector

For questions and comments about the quality of this book, please contact us at CustomerService@Harlequin.com.

Harlequin Enterprises ULC
22 Adelaide St. West, 40th Floor
Toronto, Ontario M5H 4E3, Canada
www.Harlequin.com

Printed in U.S.A.

Two-time RITA® Award nominee and Golden Quill award winner **Jennifer Morey** writes single-title contemporary romance and page-turning romantic suspense. She has a geology degree and has managed export programs in compliance with the International Traffic in Arms Regulations (ITAR) for the aerospace industry. She lives at the foot of the Rocky Mountains in Denver, Colorado, and loves to hear from readers through her website, jennifermorey.com, or Facebook.

Books by Jennifer Morey

Harlequin Romantic Suspense

Cold Case Detectives

A Wanted Man
Justice Hunter
Cold Case Recruit
Taming Deputy Harlow
Runaway Heiress
Hometown Detective
Cold Case Manhunt
Her P.I. Protector

The Coltons of Mustang Valley

Colton Family Bodyguard

The Coltons of Roaring Springs

Colton's Convenient Bride

The Coltons of Red Ridge

Colton's Fugitive Family

Visit Jennifer's Author Profile page at Harlequin.com, or jennifermorey.com, for more titles.

To my Bumblebee,
the bravest man I've ever known.

Chapter 1

The rain had cleared out overnight, leaving the April morning damp and cool. Water dripped off trees and trickled through the stable downspouts. Birds chirped and sunlight painted the horizon a stunning orange and pink. Skylar Chelsey's cowgirl boots crunched over the soggy gravel lane that led to the stable and other outbuildings.

Skylar opened the double door and found Shawn Bellarmine, her deputy ranch manager, talking with one of the grooms. Marko Darcey had just finished saddling Sir Bogie, her roan gelding. Her father had hired Shawn before Skylar had taken over the overall management of the ranch. He was experienced and reliable, but hadn't been happy when he'd essentially been demoted when Skylar took over.

"I'll get to the other horses now that I'm finished here," Marko said.

Shawn saw Skylar and stopped whatever he was about to say to the groom.

Had he tried to get Marko to drop what he was doing to obey him?

"Good morning," she said to both of them.

Marko smiled with genuine respect and Shawn just mumbled, "Mornin'."

"Thank you," she said to the groom, taking Bogie's reins. Then she turned to Shawn. "Is everything all right?"

"Just fine, ma'am."

The groom went to a nearby stall and got busy feeding the animals.

"I'm going to check the cattle in the south pasture and then ride the fence." She climbed onto the roan.

"I've got an errand to run and then I'll be back. You hear from your brother?" Shawn asked.

He rarely engaged in conversation with her, so, halting Bogie, she turned to look back at him. "No. Should I have?"

"Ran into him last night at your parents'. He looked worn and well into a few glasses of spirits. I asked the housekeeper if he was all right and she said his wife kicked him out of the house—she heard him talking to your father. Apparently, Ambrosia wants everything and then some. She's going to clean him out." Shawn emitted a single laugh, clearly enjoying the news.

Skylar's brother deserved what he got, after marrying a woman like Ambrosia. Everyone other than Corbin had seen that she'd only been interested in his money.

"Corbin was surprised?" she asked.

"I'd say he was more upset than surprised. He must have loved her."

"*Thought* he loved her," Skylar corrected, not feeling very sorry for Corbin. It was high time he wised up when it came to women and started choosing much more carefully. She'd talk to him later. Maybe. Corbin liked to turn those kinds of topics back around onto her, pointing out her failures when it came to men. He never admitted that she'd learned from her mistakes and he had yet to. She'd had some doozies, though. She could never recognize men who wanted her for her money and nothing more until she had invested too much of her heart, for one.

She guided Bogie out of the stable and rode toward the pasture. It was just a little bit out of the way to the River Rock Ranch—also known as the "Triple R"—property perimeter.

She loved these rides; the early Texas morning, the quiet, other than the happily chirping birds, the sight of livestock beginning their day, and bonding with Bogie. He was an intelligent horse that, she swore, understood everything she said. He definitely knew her moods and sometimes took advantage of that, like when she was tired. He'd bolt into a run if he felt the urge. When she was feeling low, he always comforted her by nudging her with his soft, velvety nose and nickering gently. His golden-brown eyes were windows into a mighty soul.

Skylar thought about her brother's forthcoming divorce. Skylar took the position that rushing into a union wasn't smart. Corbin argued that being with someone was better than being without. Skylar didn't mind being alone.

After seeing the cattle were fine, she headed for the river that ran through the Chelsey property and meandered into the adjacent land. About twenty minutes later, she reached it. Her neighbors, Weston and Charlotte McKann, ran a horse boarding and training operation on the adjacent ranch, and they pretty much kept to themselves. The only times Skylar had spoken with Wes had been over fence issues and roaming livestock.

Movement ahead attracted her attention. She saw a person working in a group of trees just on the other side of the fence. It appeared to be a man. He was a fair distance away, but Skylar could tell he was digging. Something lying on the ground beside him—an elongated black plastic bag or tarp rolled up, with something inside—made her pull Bogie to a stop. The man saw her and stopped shoveling.

Skylar felt a prickle of foreboding on her neck. She couldn't explain the cause of the sensation. She had no way of knowing what he was doing, or why he was digging in such an odd location—far from any buildings or people.

Was that Wes? He wore a cowboy hat and seemed about the right height and build, but she couldn't be sure. She nudged Bogie forward. As soon as she did, the man dropped his shovel and walked toward a gray car. Reaching inside, he came out with a pistol.

Alarmed, Skylar wheeled Bogie and then kicked him into a full run. Bogie charged in the direction of the River Rock stable.

"Hea! Hea!" she shouted. Bogie extended his stride farther. Skylar heard the gun go off and waited in pure terror for a bullet to rip through her. Nothing. Bogie was blowing hard and Skylar could feel his muscles strain at their limits as though he sensed the danger.

As they neared the trees that lined the river, the man fired at her again. This time Skylar saw the bullet strike the ground beside Bogie's hooves. The gelding whinnied in fear and surged even faster.

They reached the trees. Skylar didn't have to guide Bogie; he maneuvered between trunks with smooth and graceful power.

Skylar dared to look behind them. She could no longer see the man but didn't take any chances that he might try to chase her. Urging Bogie to charge over a hill, Skylar spotted the River Rock outbuildings and a surge of guarded relief flooded her. She wasn't in the clear yet. Or, at least, she couldn't be sure just yet. With Bogie galloping at breakneck speed, she just might make it. Turning her head to look behind her, she still saw no sign of the shooter. Facing forward, she gently slowed the gelding.

"It's okay now, Bogie." She stroked his now steaming neck to reassure him.

The big roan slowed as they neared the stable. A few ranch hands working in the corral and between outbuildings stopped to watch.

Bogie jarred to a stop at the stable gate, breathing heavily and sporting a gleam of sweat.

"Are you all right?" Marko asked, leaving the yearling he'd been working with in the training pen and running toward her.

"Call the sheriff! Someone just shot at me." She dismounted and reached up to pet Bogie's head. Eyes still wide and nostrils flared, he looked her way and calmed some. "It's okay, Bogie."

The groom pulled out his mobile phone and made the call.

Skylar let her forehead fall against the horse's neck, her own heart beginning to ease its frantic pace. "Thank you, Bogie." If not for him, she would have been shot and likely killed. If that man was willing to shoot at her, he must have been up to something terrible, something he meant to hide. And if he thought she could expose him, would he keep coming after her? Surely he wouldn't chase her all the way here and risk being seen. Still, she'd be looking over her shoulder until the man was caught.

Hearing a pickup, she moved back and saw that her brother Cal had just arrived. He had flown out with his new wife, Jaslene, for a family visit—something he had been doing more often now. Jaslene stepped out of the passenger seat, along with someone else from the back of the king cab that Skylar didn't recognize.

"Working the horses extra today?" Cal quipped as he got out and stepped around the truck. He must have noticed her expression and sobered. "What happened?"

Her heart still slammed in her chest. "Someone shot at me when I went on a fence-check ride." She gathered Bogie's reins to hand him over to Marko.

Cal searched around as Jaslene came to stand next him. The stranger stood to his left.

"Shot at you? Why?" Cal demanded as Jaslene said at the same time, "Oh my gosh, are you okay?"

"I saw him digging just on the other side of our fence. There was something rolled up in black plastic on the ground," she said. "It looked like a body."

Cal turned to look at the stranger beside him. "I'd say we should search the property, but the gunman is probably long gone by now."

"If it's a body, he'll have to load it back into his car," Skylar said. "He left it there when he chased me." He also hadn't chased her long. "He probably has a ten-minute head start, fifteen by the time we get there in a vehicle."

"That's enough time for him to get away," Cal said.

"The sheriff should be on his way by now," Skylar said, looking at the groom, who nodded.

The stranger looked at her. Despite what she'd just been through, she couldn't help but return his studying glance. He was a tall glass of sweet tea, with thick, dark, sandy-blond hair and Caribbean-blue eyes. Fit and muscular, he wore dark slacks with a blue-and-white print dress shirt and a black tie. He was clean-cut and citified, not the type that normally caught her eye. But there was something about him that kept her attention. Maybe it was his direct way of looking back at her. Or his unreadability. Probably both, along with the way he moved, unhurried and with a slight sway of his masculine shoulders.

"Julien LaCroix." The handsome man held out his hand to her. "Are you all right?"

He almost made everything all right just by looking at him, she thought to herself. "Yes."

"This is an old friend from my time as a Texas Ranger," Cal said, nodding at Julien. "He's a co-worker of mine now."

"And you never told me about him?" Skylar turned to her brother, who worked as a P.I. at Dark Alley Investigations.

Cal had drifted away from the family for a while; she supposed his meeting and marrying Jaslene had had a lot to do with that. Cal had helped her solve her friend's murder and, during the course of the investigation, they had fallen in love.

The sheriff's Jeep appeared on the property and came to a stop near them. Skylar felt a wave of relief, just the sight of law enforcement giving her a sense of safety.

"I'll take care of Bogie," Marko said.

"He needs extra care after what we just went through," she said, handing him the reins.

"I love taking care of this one." The groom petted Bogie's muscular neck and led him off toward the stable.

The sheriff, a big man with a big girth, took lumbering strides as he walked toward them.

"I'm Sheriff McKenzie. Someone called in a shooting?" he said.

Skylar explained in as much detail as she could what had happened.

"I'll take a drive out there to see what I can find. Can you tell me where?"

"I can show you," Skylar said.

"We'll go with you." Cal motioned to Julien. "I'll drive."

"If we see anything like that gunman still out there, stay back," the sheriff warned, pulling down his cowboy hat.

Jaslene followed Cal and Julien to the truck. "Don't even try to get me to stay here." She got into the front passenger seat and Skylar hopped in beside Julien in the back of the cab.

"Where to?" Cal asked.

Skylar told him and the sheriff followed behind. They rode down the long driveway leading from the ranch buildings to the two-lane highway. After passing the driveway to Skylar's house—which was also on the ranch property—she told Julien to take a right onto a dirt road that followed the River Rock Ranch fence. A few minutes later, she told Cal to stop when they reached the spot where she'd seen the gunman. But now the car and the rolled black plastic were both gone. That came as no surprise to her. Of course he would try to cover his tracks.

Alighting from the truck, Skylar walked toward the area where she had seen the bag or tarp. Spotting the disturbed ground ahead, she stopped and pointed. The man must have refilled the hole he had been digging.

"Stay back. I'm going to call in crime scene investigators." The sheriff started to tape off the area around the disturbed soil.

Skylar rubbed her arms. Knowing a body wouldn't be found, if that's what the man had intended to bury, she couldn't help but wonder. What would the sheriff find?

Julien waited in Cal's parents' spacious and bright kitchen. Cal had told him Jaslene was in her first trimester of pregnancy and had gone up to take a nap. He couldn't stop looking at Skylar. He'd tried to keep his gawking to a minimum, but he found her so attractive that he feared she had already noticed. He knew Cal had—he'd glanced over during one of Julien's "spells" and done something of a double-take.

It wasn't often a woman captured Julien's attention this way. Skylar appealed to everything he liked physically in a woman. Her long, thick black hair was up in a low ponytail and she had taken off her Stetson hat. In a flannel shirt, jeans and cowgirl boots, she may as well have been a in low-cut evening gown with all her curves. And those eyes… *Damn.* He could stare into their dark blue depths for an hour and still not get tired of doing so.

But he never mixed work with romance and he was ultra choosy about the women he did see. None of them ever lasted very long. He knew what he wanted in a woman and in a family. He would not get that part of his life wrong. He'd come close in the past. Never again… Not even if Skyler was one of the most alluring women he'd ever met—and in need of his help.

"What are you working on?" Cal asked. "Besides my sister?"

Cal would tease him in front of her. He noticed Skylar look at him.

Cal worked in a satellite office in Chesterville, West Virginia, and they hadn't had time to catch up on their work lives. Cal and Jaslene had just arrived in Texas for a visit with Cal's family today. Cal had invited Julien to join him and his wife. They picked him up after landing at the airport. Julien had joined them to save time. Cal couldn't stay long.

"A missing person case. A fourteen-year-old boy didn't come home from school three days ago. No leads. His grandmother hired DAI because she feels the police aren't doing enough."

"Maybe he ditched class and something happened," Cal said.

"That's what I thought. His parents said it wouldn't be the first time he'd ditched. He's a troubled teen, been arrested for robbery, and was suspended from school last year."

"What's his family like?" Skylar asked.

Julien welcomed the excuse to look into her beautiful eyes again. "Not very stable. The mother doesn't work and the stepfather works when he isn't fired from job to job. His grandmother said his stepfather drinks a lot of beer. She's tried to get her grandson to live with her, but the parents refused."

"That's so sad," she said. "Why hasn't the state taken the boy away from them?"

"No evidence of abuse or neglect."

A housekeeper had let someone in the front door. Julien turned with Cal and Skylar to see the sheriff approach. He and his team had been gone for about four hours. The sheriff took out a cell phone and showed them a photo of a simple trash bag sitting beside a hole in the ground—where Skylar had seen the man digging.

"Garbage? That's not what I saw," Skylar said.

"It's what was buried there," the sheriff said.

"I saw something wrapped in an elongated piece of black plastic, or a tarp, not a trash bag," Skylar insisted, sounding upset.

Julien reached over and put his hand on her shoulder, an impulse that made him too aware of how much he wanted to protect her. And how attracted to her he was.

"We searched for other evidence and found none. No casings, no blood, no murder weapon of any kind."

Sheriff McKenzie's tone implied he didn't believe Skylar.

"Someone *shot at me!*" she insisted.

"I didn't find any proof of that. We looked."

Skylar folded her arms in offense.

"He could have picked up the casings and buried the trash bag to cover his tracks," Julien said.

"That may be, but without proof, there's not a whole lot I can do at this point." The sheriff turned back to Skylar. "I'm not saying no one shot at you, miss."

He was just saying he couldn't do anything. But Julien could.

"Thanks for checking," Julien said. He glanced at Cal, who nodded.

The sheriff headed for the door.

"Wait a minute." Skylar followed him. "So that's it? Someone shoots at me and because there is no evidence, case closed? Are you serious?"

Julien came to stand before her. "I'll take it from here, Skylar." She sure was a feisty one.

She stared at him as though uncomprehending. He could hear her thinking, *How the heck can he take it from here?*

"Sorry I couldn't do more." The sheriff touched the brim of his hat in farewell, but gave Skylar a dubious look before he turned.

Cal walked into the entryway.

Julien watched Skylar pivot from the departing sheriff and look at her brother expectantly. She must know he was a good detective, he thought, and was waiting for him to tell her what he was going to do.

"We'll find the shooter," Julien said, bringing Skylar's head toward him.

"We will, Skylar," Cal reassured her. "Nobody messes with my little sister and gets away with it."

"I thought you had to get back to West Virginia," Skylar said.

"Yes, a case just came through. We need to fly back tonight."

She seemed disappointed but apparently understood. "All right." Next, she slid a tentative glance to Julien.

"You'll be in good hands with Julien. He wouldn't be working for DAI if he wasn't one of the best," Cal told her. "And I'd give the case to someone else if I didn't have the utmost confidence in him."

Nothing like a little pressure.

After a moment, Skylar shook her head and, with a sigh, wiped a few strands of hair off her forehead. "All right. I'm going to go check on Bogie and then go home for the rest of the day."

It was well into the afternoon now. Skylar hugged her brother.

"I'll be in touch," Cal said as she withdrew.

Skylar turned to Julien and, after her eyes roamed his face, she extended her hand.

He took it for a semi shake. Not too tight, not too

soft. His defenses went up over the way she looked at him. *Take it nice and slow*, he told himself. No time for romance until he solved her mystery.

"I wish we could have met under difference circumstances," he said.

She smiled slightly. "Yes, but I have to say I am glad we did meet."

He handed her his card, which had his office and mobile numbers.

Skylar took it. "Hang on." She hurried from the room, returning seconds later with her own business card that she must keep in her father's office. Or maybe she used it on occasion to run the ranch.

"Thanks. Call me if you notice anything odd."

"I will." With that she turned and headed for the front entrance. Julien enjoyed looking at how her jeans snugly fit her butt and the way each cheek rose and fell with her strides.

When he could no longer see her, he turned to Cal. His friend had noticed the observation and looked amused.

"I should warn you that she's stubborn and loud."

"Okay." Stubborn was all right as long as it wasn't malicious.

"She's accustomed to running everything on her own," Cal continued.

"Okay." Might be a good complement to the hours he worked.

"She was raised by my dad. I didn't listen to his preaching as much as she did."

Julien had to pause at that one. "She doesn't seem greedy. Is she?"

"I wouldn't say 'greedy,' but the bottom line is important to her."

That didn't sound too harmful. Besides, he didn't even know her yet. He only knew she was a knockout and he was very attracted to that. He'd take his time getting to know her.

"No man has ever lasted with her," Cal went on.

"Does she have any redeeming qualities in your mind?" Julien had to ask.

Cal chuckled. "Everything I said except her thirst for a high bottom line." He paused, as though thinking. "That and her love of nature and animals. And she does stand up to Dad. He doesn't dare tell her how to run the ranch anymore. He works too much to do it himself and Dad can't boss her around like he could his other ranch managers."

Julien felt a spark of excitement over the prospect of engaging a woman like that. A love of nature and animals spoke of a softer side. He liked independent women, too. Independence meant she'd be more likely to tolerate a man with a career like his, where the hours ran long and unpredictable.

With his thoughts rambling way too far into the future, Julien checked himself. He'd help her stay safe from the gunman and try to uncover what she'd seen him doing first. Anything personal had to wait. His usual resolve on that point wavered, though. He felt doubt and began to worry he might not be able to resist his attraction to Skylar.

Chapter 2

Skylar had gotten an early start after taking yesterday off—well, sort of. Being chased by a madman and then dealing with the sheriff hadn't exactly been a day off. She'd needed the down time after that, but it hadn't alleviated her tension. She'd taken a ranch hand with her on her ride around the perimeter, looking behind her every so often, half expecting to see the gunman coming after her. Tired and hungry—she'd skipped lunch and now it was going on three—she contemplated going home to grab a sandwich and take a bath with candles and bubbles.

She walked toward her truck and then she saw Julien waiting there. He smiled a little, almost a grin, and her lips turned up involuntarily. She came to a stop before him.

"I thought I'd come by and check on you," he said.

"Do I need checking?"

"I need it. To see for myself that you're all right."

Did he care because she was Cal's little sister or for another reason?

"I also wanted to let you know I made arrangements to speak with Wes McKann and thought you might want to go with me."

"You had to make arrangements?"

"I wasn't able to catch him at home when I stopped by last evening. He was reluctant to meet with me when I phoned him early this morning. I had to tell him eventually I'd find probable cause and allow the police to get a warrant. He told me to come by this afternoon."

"'Probable cause'?" That got her attention.

"His wife went missing a few days ago. After I left here, I did some digging. There are three missing person cases in this county. One is my missing boy. The other is McCann's wife, Charlotte. And the third is the wife of a lawyer. Haven't talked to him yet."

"All missing? Isn't that a lot?"

Julien shrugged and looked out across the ranch land, squinting his eyes slightly. "Concentrated in this area?" He met her eyes again. "Maybe. Two women in the same county has me very suspicious. The missing teen being related doesn't seem possible."

He thought the two women could be linked? "What do you know about the lawyer?"

"Nothing yet." He checked his watch. "Can you take a break for an hour or so?"

"I'm finished for the day." She walked with him toward a dark blue BMW X5. He drove a nice vehicle. Not a pickup like many men did, but a sophisticated SUV.

At the BMW, she was startled when he reached past her and opened the passenger door for her.

Turning her head, she saw his smiling eyes and felt a tingle chase through her. "I can't remember the last time a man opened a door for me." She hoped the faint breathlessness in her voice wasn't obvious.

"You must not date much."

She smiled back at him. She didn't date very much.

Getting into the BMW, she watched Julien walk around to the other side, admiring his graceful but sturdy gait and the sway of his powerful shoulders.

He got in, started the SUV and they were on their way. She was aware of him sitting only a few feet from her, and wondered if Julien was as aware of her, too.

"So, do you?" he asked.

"Do I what?"

"Date much."

Leave it to a P.I. to turn an uncomfortable situation into an opportunity to learn something about a woman, she thought, but said, "In my experience, most men don't like a woman in charge." And she would do the same with him. How would he respond to her statement? She always liked to find out early on. Then she didn't have to waste time going on a date with a man she knew wouldn't be compatible.

"In my experience, most women don't like a man who isn't around much."

Huh. She hadn't heard that one before. "My work is important to me, too."

He turned his head to glance at her and she thought she saw surprise in his eyes.

"Do we have something in common?" she asked.

"A rarity for sure."

For him? she wondered.

He parked in front of Wes McCann's two-story Colonial and they walked to the front door, which opened before they got there. Skylar felt awkward about accompanying Julien here, but he had insisted to ensure her safety.

Wes McCann was a ruggedly handsome man if a woman could get past his bristly nature. He was slightly taller than Julien's six-two, with jet-black hair that peeked out from under his black cowboy hat, and piercing blue eyes that held no welcome.

"What's she doing here?" Wes demanded.

"She's part of the reason I'm here."

"Nice to see you, Mr. McCann." Skylar stepped into the home ahead of Julien as Wes moved to let them pass.

"What does my wife's disappearance have to do with her?" Wes asked Julien.

Skylar stood next to him in the wide, wood-floored foyer.

"Would you mind telling me when you last saw your wife?" Julien asked.

"I already told the sheriff everything I know."

"Wasn't it one of your wife's friends who actually reported her missing?"

That question fell on Wes abrasively and his eyes hardened in warning. "Yes."

"Why didn't you report her missing?"

"Charlotte frequently goes on trips without telling me. She usually goes to her parents' house in Maine. That's why I wasn't concerned. I didn't know she wasn't there until after her friend reported her missing. Apparently this friend called and discovered she wasn't there."

He sounded believable. But Skylar couldn't be sure he wasn't the same man she saw digging a hole. She told the sheriff he had been too far away to describe reliably.

"How was your marriage, Mr. McCann?" Julien asked.

Skylar remained quiet, letting the professional do all the questioning, even though she wondered the same. She was with Julien to be safe, not solve a case.

Wes looked from Julien to Skylar and then back at Julien. "Why are you asking me questions about my wife?" He nodded his head at Skylar. "What does she have to do with her disappearance?" Then he looked right at her with those unnerving eyes. "Do you know what happened to her?"

"No."

"She saw someone digging a hole next to your property line yesterday," Julien said.

Wes's eyes softened but shrewdness took over as he turned once again to Skylar. "Oh, I get it. The sheriff came by and told me about that. You think I tried to bury my wife there." He chuckled, but not in a humorous way. "You both can go now. If you need to ask me more questions, you're going to have to have me arrested." He went to the door and opened it.

"We mean no disrespect, Mr. McCann," Skylar said. "Do you know who may have dug a hole and put a bag of trash in it?"

"No, I don't," he replied curtly, extending his hand palm-up in an invitation for them to leave.

Skylar moved to stand in front of him. "A man shot at me when I saw him digging."

"It wasn't me," Wes insisted.

"You own a gun, don't you?" she asked, ignoring his arrogant tone.

"I own several," he shot back, as though she should know better.

But that was not why she had asked.

"What kind?" Julien asked.

"I don't have to answer any of these questions."

"Where were you yesterday morning?" Skylar asked.

"Working my ranch."

"Can anyone confirm that?" Julien asked.

"I prefer to work alone. Now, if you *don't mind*?" Wes ground out the last words, clearly reaching his limit of patience.

Julien placed his hand on Skylar's lower back. "Let's go."

She passed the glowering Mr. McCann and walked with Julien to his SUV, where he once again opened the door for her. She got in and looked toward the house, seeing Wes staring at them from the open entry. She continued to watch him stare as Julien drove away, facing forward only when she could no longer see Wes.

"He's an angry man," she said.

"Yeah. Defensive."

Because he was guilty? "He said Charlotte frequently left without telling him."

"Not a sign of a happy marriage."

"Maybe she left him for good this time. Maybe she doesn't want to be found," Skylar said. "A man like that would scare away most women. Living with one would be infinitely worse."

"Maybe she left and he found her," Julien said. "I checked for credit card activity and didn't find any."

She knew what he meant. Maybe Wes had found her and killed her.

Skylar rubbed her arms as goose bumps spread across her skin.

After Julien dropped her off at home, Skylar finally could take a long, hot, candle-lit bath. She added a nice glass of Pinot Grigio to the time. Putting the glass on the windowsill beside the tub, she stepped into the lavender-scented water, the bath bomb still fizzing at the bottom. Sinking into the water, she sighed and leaned her head back against a folded towel.

The sound of the television she'd left on downstairs kept her company along with the ever-lingering thoughts of Julien. When he'd dropped her off, he'd walked her to her door. At first, she assumed he did so as a romantic gesture, but then she'd seen him looking around for any signs of something amiss. She also recalled he'd done that all the way to her house, looking in his rearview mirror, at side roads and people they passed. The drop of disappointment in her stomach had surprised her.

What had she expected? For him to kiss her? She didn't even know him. All she knew about him was that he was Cal's close friend from the past and that he'd had similar experiences with women as she'd had with men.

That, and he was gorgeous.

So, she was physically attracted to him. She didn't know enough to jump into anything yet. She had to stop jumping into relationships.

Reaching over to pick up her glass of wine, the sound of something breaking downstairs stopped her.

What was that? A glass? She had not left anything on the counters in the kitchen. A window? Alarm sent chills up her spine.

Skylar stood and stepped out of the tub, grabbing a towel for a quick dab-dry before donning her robe. Peering into her bedroom, she saw nothing out of place. At the open door to the hallway, she stopped to listen.

Some light from downstairs illuminated the hall through the open railing, but she saw no one. From downstairs she heard the ticking of the grandfather clock and the faint hum of airflow from the furnace. She heard nothing else. But she had not imagined the sound of breaking glass.

There was no landline in her room and her cell was downstairs. She looked behind her for anything that could serve as a weapon. The desk where she sometimes liked to work at night had a lamp. Too bulky. The vase might be good. But it wasn't heavy enough to smash over an intruder's head. The gas fireplace across from the foot of the bed had a poker for show. Now, *that* she could use.

She hurried to pick up the poker, then went back to her bedroom door. Checking the hall again, finding it empty and quiet, she walked slowly to the railing and peered down into her living room. The TV still played. The hall widened at the railing, the other side a den that she could close with foldable doors. She kept the doors open all the time because she liked the light. Now she was glad she did, because there was a phone in there.

She ran to the side table and lifted the receiver. No dial tone.

A shockwave of alarm sent her pulse flying. She knew someone was in the house. Someone had broken in and she didn't have to guess who.

What should she do? Find her cell phone? Get the hell out of the house?

Cell phone first.

Leaving the den, she made her way to the top of the stairs, pausing to listen. Nothing. One stair at a time, she descended. At the bottom, she could see her kitchen and living room. All was quiet.

But then she saw the back patio door. One of the French doors was open—and the glass had been shattered in one of the panels.

Skylar searched for her cell. It had been moved from the kitchen island, where she thought she'd left it, to the table. She picked it up. It was turned off. She had not turned off her phone.

She fought for calm. Panicking would not help her right now.

Sensing and then hearing an ever so slight scuff on the floor, she turned in time to see a man, dressed all in black and wearing a mask and gloves, aiming a gun at her.

Skylar dove for cover behind the kitchen island as a shot exploded. She scrambled low into the dining room, putting her back to the wall as another shot sprayed drywall. She would never get out of here if she ran. The gunman would surely shoot her before she got to the door.

She knew some self-defense moves, but not a whole lot—certainly not enough to save herself from a desperate killer. Hearing him walk toward the dining room, she waited until she could see the tip of his pistol, then stepped into the doorway at the same time she swung the poker upward, knocking the gun away. She then used one foot to slam down hard on his lower shin and rammed her knee into his groin. Next, she kicked him, sending him flying backward.

She ran for the front door, fear gripping her with each stride, expecting to be shot any second.

Before she reached the door, someone kicked it off its frame from the outside.

An instant later she saw Julien.

"Get down!" he shouted, aiming his pistol beyond her.

She dove for the floor, dropping the poker as he fired several times. Rolling onto her hip, she watched the masked man disappear into her kitchen.

Julien bolted for the other entryway to the kitchen.

Shakily getting to her feet, she heard more shots being fired. Julien had to take cover behind the living room wall but then charged into the kitchen, weapon firing. Skylar heard more shots from the backyard and then silence.

She hurried to the open, broken door, flipping on the outside lights. Julien ran toward her from the edge of trees surrounding her yard. She had no fence, so the intruder could have easily run away.

Julien reached her, putting his hands on her arms, having already holstered his gun. "Are you all right?"

She nodded, her pulse still pounding but not as frantically as when she'd thought she would be shot to death.

Julien looked back at the trees where the intruder

must have gone and then faced her again. "I would have chased him, but I was worried about you."

"I'm all right."

He guided her inside and pulled out his phone. "Do you have any wood to cover up your door?"

"I think so. I'll have one of the hands fix it tomorrow."

Julien spoke into his mobile phone to a 9-1-1 dispatcher.

Great. She'd get to endure another visit with the dubious sheriff. Except now he'd be hard-pressed to doubt her claims. Clearly she must have seen something to make the hole digger feel he needed to close loose ends.

Julien ended the call. "While we wait for the sheriff, why don't you go get dressed and pack some things? You should stay with me until we find out who tried to kill you."

He had a good point, but the notion of staying with him gave her a burst of heat. Conscious of wearing only a robe, she tightened the belt.

"I can stay with my parents," she said. "They can make sure I'm safe." Her father would probably install a robust security system complete with guards.

"You might put others in danger if you do that."

Her parents, Corbin and countless staff members might be in the line of fire if the gunman returned for another attempt.

"Then I'll beef up security here. I can't stay away from the ranch for long."

"All right, then let me help you."

"Okay." She could agree to that.

"Don't worry, I don't mix my work with pleasure," he said with a grin, giving her body a sweeping look.

"Good, then I don't have to worry about trading one danger for another." She smiled back and left him standing there, uncertainty flattening his mouth.

Chapter 3

This time the sheriff had believed Skylar had seen something nefarious. The sheriff would do his own investigation, but Julien could help. She'd allowed him to stay the night but this morning she had left early to begin her day. She'd promised to keep her deputy manager nearby, but Julien was still worried. He'd reluctantly had to leave to work on his other cases, but not before putting a GPS tracker in Skylar's truck and arranging for repairs on her house. He hadn't had a chance to tell her, she'd left in such a hurry. He would tell her later. Right now, he was tracking her to a farm and ranch supply store. Not liking the thought of her out of his sight, he drove there and waited outside.

When she appeared with a cart full of things, he left his SUV and walked toward her truck. She saw him and stopped at the tailgate.

"What are you doing here?" she asked.

"I've been tracking your movements. Sorry for not telling you. I meant to." He lifted a heavy bag of horse feed supplements.

"Should I be worried about the invasion of my privacy?"

That he was tracking her? "No. You should feel safer. Is your door fixed?"

"Yes, along with all the bullet holes. Thanks for doing that. You didn't have to."

"I know. I wanted to"

"You should have told me you were watching me. I would have been all right with that. It's for my safety. Right now I feel stalked." She put a bedding fork in the back and he put the last feed supplement there.

"Sorry. I'm tracking you with GPS. There are devices in the truck and in your wallet."

She looked down at her purse, which hung diagonally over her shoulder and hip.

He put some tack in the truck.

Finished loading the truck, she closed the tailgate and faced him. "What else have you done?"

"Not as much as I'd like to." Although he hadn't

meant the double entendre, his eyes raked down her body.

When he returned his gaze to hers, he caught her finishing her own appreciative observation. He grinned.

Her mouth curved upward slightly.

"What I meant is I'd rather be near you 24/7 to protect you. That attack proves how vulnerable you are," he said.

"I know what you meant." Her soft smile remained as she seemed to consider something else. "I don't let men I just met move in with me."

"I wouldn't be moving in. I'd be a houseguest for a while. Separate bedrooms."

Her smile slowly eased away but a flirtatious light glinted in her eyes. "Why don't we start with dinner? Then I'll decide."

The invitation surprised him. She must know she was in significant danger. A killer had attacked her in her own home. Maybe she kept it light by using dinner as an excuse to give in. Or maybe these sparks flying between them had more to do with that.

"Dinner it is." He'd be sure to pack a bag, too, because he fully planned on sticking around to make sure she was safe.

Skylar brooded over her invitation. She had clearly gotten lost in flirtation. She'd blurted it before thinking. She had been worried about living alone and whether the attacker would strike again. At the time she'd suggested dinner, she'd thought, Why not? She'd told herself she'd done it with her safety in mind. But she could not fool herself. Having Julien over for dinner excited her.

Without knowing anything about his taste in food, she had opted for surf and turf. A couple of juicy steaks and crab legs with scalloped potatoes and a salad. With the water heating for the crab and the steaks seasoned and ready for the grill, the doorbell rang.

"Right on time." She opened the door to see Julien in slacks and a dress shirt. Nice but casual. She'd decided the same, wearing black leggings and a white-and-black-patterned shirt that flowed past her hips.

"Hi," she said.

"Hi." With a sexy, crooked grin, he stepped inside.

Telling herself this was not a date and calming the arousing heat the sight of him gave her, she closed and locked the door.

"I hope you like steak and crab." She led him into her house, seeing how he checked the place out, and not out of admiration. He looked for security.

"The only thing I don't like is roasted beetles."

She laughed as she entered the kitchen. "Is that a real thing?"

"Supposedly they're a salty snack."

Skylar felt like gagging. "Yuck."

He chuckled as she retrieved the steak from the refrigerator.

"Would you like some wine while you grill these for me?" she asked.

"Sure."

She handed him the plate of raw, seasoned meat and then went to her wine cooler, selecting a good white. She brought the filled glasses out to the back patio, setting his down on the stone counter of her built-in barbecue. She took a seat on the outdoor couch and put her glass on the coffee table. She had already lit some tiki torches and the soft lights strung along the top rim of the gazebo.

After lighting the grill, he let it heat and came over to sit beside her. "This is nice."

"As a lover of the outdoors, I had to have a patio I could practically live on."

"I'm a lover of barbecues."

Maybe he wasn't such a city boy after all. She'd like to get to know him more. "You never did tell me if you and my brother planned on joining DAI together. You must be really good friends."

"We are. Well, we were until he got married and moved."

"No." She inwardly laughed imagining him as one.

"Your brother and I worked together as Rangers

until he got married and moved. He joined DAI before me," he said, finally answering her question. "We were always a lot alike. We met in college, both of us getting criminal justice degrees. I think we had a fascination with superheroes, but your grandfather's murder ultimately made him decide to become a detective." He stopped and seemed to ponder something before he finally said, "I have always wanted to fight bad guys."

Skylar strongly suspected there was more to it than he'd revealed, but didn't question him.

"Cal and I both aspired to fight bad guys, but after college, we were still young and wild with no focused direction. We became troopers and then Rangers. He moved away. Then there was this murder in Irving that hit too close to home. I helped solve it. That's when Cal introduced me to Kadin Tandy. He lost his daughter to violent crime and founded Dark Alley Investigations."

"It seems like a lot of the agency's investigators have lost someone." Curiosity gnawed at her. She wanted so much to ask if he had lost someone, too, but didn't want to overstep.

"Yes," he said quietly.

Skylar wouldn't get too personal. She would be patient.

"Are you from Irving?" she asked, noticing how he'd relaxed, tension easing. She had always been intuitive with people. Maybe that came from being raised by someone like her father. She had learned at a young age how to gauge him so she knew when to stay off his radar.

"Fredericksburg. My family still lives there. I moved to Dallas. My parents run a wildflower seed farm and my sister manages the operations."

Skylar had heard of Fredericksburg. A town with German influence, it was in the Texas Hill Country, about an hour or two drive from the Chelsey ranch, which was just north of Irving.

"A wildflower seed farm?" How fascinating. "You must have interesting parents."

He smiled, big and genuine. Right away Skylar knew he was close to his parents. Her immediate thought was that she never smiled like that when people asked her about her parents.

"They are. They are smart, happy people who were meant for each other. Two of the lucky ones who met their soul mate and raised kids the right way."

Skylar did love her parents but she could never say they were soul mates. She was pretty sure her mother had married her father because of his position in society and his earning potential.

"My sister and I were brought up with positive influence," Julien said, sounding proud. "Our parents believed in us earning privileges. They had us work the farm, which they called our chores, but as I grew up, I realized that was intentional. My dad would always teach us things, not just tasks that had to be done in running a farm or any other business, but integrity and the importance of having good principles."

He seemed to fall into fond memories and Skylar was envious. "I asked him once where he learned to be such a good parent and he told me 'from having bad ones.'" Julien's brief laugh was full of affection. "His father—my grandfather—was an alcoholic who mistreated my grandmother. They're both gone now, but I never spent much time with them. My dad didn't like having them around. My mother's parents were much different. They came for every holiday. I also think my dad learned how to be a good parent from them—and my mother, since she was raised pretty much the same way."

Skylar sipped her wine, loving hearing the story about his obviously wonderful family.

"I'm talking a lot. Sorry," he said.

"No. It's fine. I'm enchanted."

He looked at her in a way that seemed appreciative but was likely more along the lines of attraction.

"Is your sister younger or older than you?" she asked.

"She's younger by three years. She's engaged to be married at the end of summer. My parents are ecstatic."

Skylar wouldn't doubt it. They probably looked

forward to grandchildren in whom they could instill integrity. She thought of her parents, and how different they were, and it seemed suddenly comical.

She breathed a laugh. "My parents were nothing like that."

Julien smiled without showing any teeth. "Her fiancé's dad owns the hardware store in town."

"So, he's set financially. Is that important to your parents?"

"Her security is important, not just the money by itself. He had to pass the integrity and principle test."

Skylar marveled over that for a second. "Wow. My dad doesn't care about that. He'd railroad anyone who got in his way of success. I think my brother Corbin is the same way. I keep wondering if there's hope for him, but his track record with women suggests not."

"What about you?"

Was he asking if she would railroad anyone to achieve success? "I like to think I'd pass your father's integrity and principle test, but I wasn't raised by wholesome parents." No, she'd been raised by rich and affluent parents. Her father hadn't just made a lot of money working, he had inherited most of his wealth.

"Surely there had to be good times."

There had been, thanks to her mother, but her dad hadn't been home much. "My dad told us if we dated anyone lazy or got addicted to anything disreputable, he'd disown us. He instilled in us the need to work hard. I suppose that's good in some ways. And it could have been worse." While her parents had never mistreated them, Skylar had never felt comfortable going to them for serious talks. She had done that with friends.

"Someday, I want what my parents had," Julien said.

He wanted a wholesome family. Love with a woman—a soul mate—and children.

Skylar had never considered raising a family. In fact, she had always felt a bit of a disconnect with women who wanted to have babies. She had never felt that desire. Maybe that was because of how she was raised.

After several seconds thinking that over, she met Julien's eyes and saw him closely regarding her. He must have accurately assessed her reaction. He must also know having children was not on her bucket list.

"Did you have animals on the farm?" she asked him. Maybe they had something in common there.

"Dogs and cats. Nothing like what you have here. My childhood was idyllic but I was so sick of working on the farm that I couldn't wait to live in the city. Now that I've been there several years, I know that's where I belong."

Scratch that. Maybe they had nothing in common other than him keeping her safe. "I love animals and ranching."

She met his look and felt his silent agreement that they had very different lifestyle preferences. And *that* was too significant to ignore. Sexually attracted or not, they wouldn't last as a couple. If anything happened between them, it would be casual and temporary. He must be thinking along the same lines because his eyes grew hooded with enticement.

"How about those steaks?" she said, breaking the awkward moment.

Julien had just finished helping Skylar clean the kitchen and still wasn't sure how he felt about her passion for ranching. As soon as he'd graduated from high school, he'd left the wildflower seed farm. While he kept in contact with his family and visited them often, he loved the noise and busyness of the Dallas area. And most of all, he loved solving crimes, bringing the scourge of society to justice.

They'd shared small talk through dinner, which had actually been nice. He'd found he could be with her, not talk about anything ultra significant, and yet remain like-minded. They'd had comfortable lapses in conversation, too. Comfortable. How weird was that? Before dinner, he'd thought they wouldn't stand a chance as a couple—he couldn't live on a ranch and she would never live in the city. How would that work?

Skylar made tea and joined him in the living room, sitting beside him on the sofa. He took a cup and saucer, noting the indigo peony pattern of the delicate china. He had noticed other unique touches in her house. Some vintage decorative pieces, color-coordinated paintings, other ornamentals and lighting in all the right places and at soothing brightness.

Seeing the home décor magazines and books on the coffee table, he began to wonder. "Did you do all this?" he asked, gesturing around him with his free hand.

"Yes. When I was a kid, I wanted to be an interior designer."

That was new, something he hadn't expected, but seemingly way off course from her ranching career.

"Why didn't you become one?"

She shrugged. "When I was seventeen, I told my mother I wanted to go to college to learn interior design," she said. "The next night when my dad came home from work, he came to my room and said Mom told him about my plans. He then proceeded to inform me that no Chelsey got a job like that."

Julien lifted his brow. "He said that?"

"That's my dad. Reputation and social status are everything to him. He said only stupid women work as interior designers. He said my playing as a child with designing dollhouses was adorable, but I was old enough to decide on a satisfactory career."

"And you didn't defy him?" She struck him as the kind of woman who would, but at seventeen she may have been too impressionable.

"No one defies Newman Chelsey," she said, looking away.

This was getting interesting. Here he had thought she was this tough cowgirl and now he could see some vulnerabilities. "Did you go to college?"

"Business," she said curtly. "I hated it."

He could see and feel her enormous regret. "Looking back, would you have become an interior designer if your father hadn't beaten you down?"

She took a couple of seconds contemplating. He spent the time absorbing her beautiful profile. Then she turned to look at him.

"No one's ever asked me that before," she said. "Especially not like that."

"I didn't mean to insult you."

She shook her head. "I'm not insulted. I'm… enlightened. Beaten me down." She nodded. "He did do that in effect. I was only seventeen and, at that time, eager to please. But, no. Ranching is not only in my blood, it's something I am very passionate about. I love all the animals. In many ways, I would rather be with them than most humans. I love interior design. It is a great hobby for me. It's a hobby, something that relaxes me, something I enjoy doing in my off time. Whether I just do some rearranging or completely redecorate a room."

So she had a creative side. And her family had so much money that she could completely redo an entire room, a whole house, whenever she wanted.

"But you would have gotten a degree in interior design," he said.

"Yes. I did take some classes and went to some conventions."

"Well, from the looks of it, you didn't need a degree. You're a natural."

She smiled her appreciation. "Thanks."

They fell into that companionable silence again, sipping tea in her pretty cups, surrounded by warm ambience.

"What made you decide to become a Ranger?" she asked.

"I always planned on becoming a detective. Being a cop was the starting point. I started out as a state trooper. Did that for eight years. By then I had experience dealing with major crimes like murder, robbery, sexual assault and fraud, so I met all the requirements. The Rangers fascinated me, and that satisfied a wild urge. Impressed the girls, too." He grinned and saw her look at his mouth, her eyes changing as they often did when she noticed him as a sexy man.

"So, when you calmed down, you joined an investigation agency?" she asked, saying *calmed down* with a note of sarcasm.

DAI hardly evoked calmness. "Something like that."

"How long were you a Ranger before you went private?" she asked.

"Almost five years. I've been with DAI for more than three years now." While a Ranger, he had discovered he felt most rewarded solving cold cases. That's why DAI suited him so well. Clients came to them when all other options had run their course. The detectives who worked there were all like him.

"You're a crusader for victims and their families," Skylar said. "You also must be really smart."

Why did she say that? "Someone has to help them."

"What's the hardest case you ever solved?" she asked, seeming genuinely interested and fascinated by his job.

He thought a moment. "There was this woman, a twenty-two-year-old, who had gone missing more than thirty years ago. Her remains were discovered, and dental records identified her, but there was no DNA evidence. No evidence at all, really. The coroner couldn't even tell us how she died. All we knew about her last days was that she'd broken up with her boyfriend and gone out to a bar the night she went missing. One of the patrons said they'd seen her leave with a man. No one could identify him.

"I looked into other missing person cases and found four that had similar circumstances—where the young girl left a bar with a man no one could identify. That took months to piece together, but it paid off." He took a short breath before continuing. "In one of the cases, a witness saw enough of the man to warrant a sketch artist. I went back to the other bars—the killer would go to bars in different counties—and showed the sketch to people who worked at the bar where my victim disappeared. A bartender identified him. Turns out, he was the ex-boyfriend of my victim. We found a bracelet in his house that she was wearing the night she went missing.

"Two of the other bodies were found and we were able to get DNA evidence linking the same killer to them. He got three life sentences without the possibility of parole."

Skylar looked at him somberly. "Like I said, you must be really smart."

"Just determined. And patient."

"And humble," Skylar said with a slight smile. "It's okay. You can admit it. You are smart. You have to be to solve thirty-year-old cases."

"Nothing a good education wouldn't prepare me for."

She gave him a soft swat on his arm. "Just say it. *Yes, I am smart.*"

He chuckled. "I did really good in college—4.0."

"Uhhh," she groaned with a lift of her eyes. "All right, that's close enough to an admission."

He looked at her pretty smile that reached her even more stunning eyes, such a deep blue with flecks of lighter shades. Her long dark hair flowed down over one shoulder. He wanted to touch the shiny strands.

Her smile slowly faded as she met his eyes, seeming to devour them the way he had devoured hers.

The gunman on the loose bothered her, and no wonder why. Julien was also troubled by that. The more time he spent with Skylar, the more important she became to him, and that made protecting her that much more urgent. He never doubted his ability to catch a bad guy, and maybe it wasn't doubt he felt right now. Maybe it was fear—fear that he would fail Skylar.

Chapter 4

Julien's chiming cell phone woke him from a restless sleep; he'd barely managed a wink, keeping one eye open for the gunman. He blinked more awake and leaned over to pick it up from the bedside table. Recognizing the number, he quickly answered.

"Indiana Deboe." A protégée of Kadin Tandy's, Indie frequently worked with Julien on cases.

"Someone called from the Tarrant County Sheriff's Office. They received a call that a boy of about fourteen stole food from a farmer's market and was seen getting on a bus headed to Fort Worth. He matches the description of your runaway," she said.

"I called the Fort Worth police and they're on the lookout for him."

"That's great news," Julien said. "Thanks, Indie."

"I hope I didn't wake you," she said teasingly. They had a running joke over the odd hours they always worked.

"You did."

"Where are you? I tried your home phone first."

"I'm working a new case. It's not really a DAI case. It's pro bono. I'm helping out Cal Chelsey's sister."

"Oh. A freebie, huh? Is she pretty?"

"Goodbye, Indie." Smiling, he hung up on her.

After showering, he went into the kitchen to find Skylar already up and ready for the day. She poured him some coffee.

"Sugar or cream? Both?"

"Neither." He took the cup from her. "Thanks." He sipped and tasted the flavored coffee. He usually drank regular coffee, but this was a nice treat. "I've got a lead on my missing boy. Can you break away for a while to go with me?"

"I've got to work all day. Can't you go yourself?"

He cocked his head at her.

"Right. A crazy man with a gun is after me. All right. I'll go talk to my ranch hands. They're going to love me today." She put down her coffee mug. "Are you hungry?"

"We can grab something on the way. We need to

hurry. A runaway on the move will be hard enough to find."

"Okay."

Julien went with her and waited for her to finish instructing her staff. They all seemed to take the extra workload positively except for one man. He could tell he was Skylar's next in command by the way she spoke to him and the orders she gave him. His name was Shawn and he epitomized what Julien imagined a cowboy to look like. Tall and lanky, wearing jeans and a flannel shirt with a cowboy hat. His face was weathered and he didn't smile at all.

Skylar thanked everyone and then walked with Julien to his BMW. He opened the passenger door for her, seeing her smile with the act of chivalry. If she kept doing that, he'd seek out other things to do for her just to see that gorgeous smile.

After Julien stopped in at the sheriff's office in Tarrant County, Skylar rode with him to the bus stop where the runaway would have gotten off. He parked.

"What do you know about the runaway? What's his name?" she asked. "Do you have a picture?" Maybe she could help. She might as well make herself useful since she now had a volunteer body-guard.

Julien reached into the back seat and pulled a case to the front. Removing his laptop, he booted up and then opened a file, turning the laptop so she could see the screen. Skylar looked into the sad brown eyes of an average-size boy with medium brown hair.

"His name is Sawyer Wilson. His friends say his parents drink a lot and are abusive. He's an only child. He does have one person who cares about him and that's his grandmother. She's been sick with cancer, though."

Skylar's heart went out to the poor boy. "What did his parents say about his disappearance?"

"Not much. They saw him get on the bus to school. He didn't give any indication he was unhappy at home. They put on a good show, but I could tell the mother felt guilty. The father smelled like whiskey."

His cell phone rang and he answered. After listening a moment, he found a pen and paper and wrote down an address.

"Indie found out Sawyer's father has a half brother who lives in Fort Worth. His name is Conner Jones," Julien said once he ended the call.

"You have some resourceful people working with you," she said.

"Yes. Lots of good people."

"Why did it take Sawyer so long to head there?"

"He may have gone somewhere else. His mother did say he saved money like a miser. He worked for his grandmother, did chores for her. Maybe he had enough money to stay in an inexpensive motel for a few nights. Some kids stay on the run until they can't feed or shelter themselves anymore."

"He must be bound and determined to get away if he traveled to Fort Worth to try to stay with an uncle who might not even want him."

"Everything I've learned about him suggests that."

This new information meant they no longer had to find witnesses who may have seen him get off the bus. Julien drove away from the bus depot and straight to the uncle's house. It made sense that the boy would go there.

Seeing Julien's concern hammered home his affection for children. It made Skylar reflect on her choices in that regard. While she had never given having a family much thought, she wondered if she should have. Given her parents hadn't taught her the value of family beyond affluence and wealth, she maybe should have looked deeper inside herself. What was wrong with having a family? Nothing. But she would want her kids to feel close to her. She was afraid she wouldn't have the skills to cultivate that kind of environment.

She glanced over at Julien. His father had probably felt the same way when he'd married his mother. But his mother had come from a good family and they'd raised Julien well.

Skylar had come from a good family in some

ways, but "loving and close" did not describe the Chelseys of River Rock Ranch.

Julien caught her contemplative look and she quickly averted her gaze.

"What were you just thinking?" he asked.

"Nothing."

After several seconds, he said, "It was something. Maybe someday you'll tell me."

That would be a heavy conversation. And one that should not take place unless the two of them entered a serious relationship. As she ran down their differences, she knew that would probably be a big mistake. Two opposites who were sexually attracted to one another might not make it a year, especially when one wanted children.

Skylar could not answer the question of whether or not she would have kids. Still, she couldn't stop thinking about how much he cared about Sawyer's welfare. He didn't have to tell her that. She could see he genuinely did. He was a hero. But he was one hero she would be smart to stay out of bed with.

Julien wanted to question Skylar on her weighty expression when she'd looked at him in the SUV. He suspected it had something to do with Sawyer. Was this the closest she had been to kids? Or caring about them?

He rang the doorbell and a slightly under-six-foot, big-bellied, bald man answered. Julien instantly smelled whiskey. Great. Sawyer had gone from one hellhole to another.

"Conner Jones?" Julien asked.

"Yeah. Who's asking?"

Julien showed his PI identification. "Julien La-Croix. I was hired by Sawyer Wilson's grandmother to find him. Is he here?"

The man breathed a sloppy sigh. "Yes. Come in."

Julien entered ahead of Skylar and checked around the messy, dirty living room. No lights were on and the trees in the front yard kept it dim.

He saw Sawyer sitting unhappily on the sofa, looking at him warily.

"I already called his father. They're on their way here. Right now," Conner said.

"The boy will be put into foster care until an investigation is complete." Julien felt an incredible compulsion to protect the boy. "When his father gets here, tell him Child Protective Services will be in contact soon."

"As long as he ain't here, I don't care." Conner turned to look at Sawyer in disgust. "What made you think I'd want you here when I have never met you in my life?" He faced Julien again. "I hate my half brother. We never talk. What was this kid thinking?"

"He was thinking anywhere is better than his home. He was thinking maybe he'd have a better life with you," Julien said, getting angry.

"Let's go, Sawyer." Skylar held out her hand to the boy.

Her interjection surprised Julien. For a woman who claimed she didn't want kids, she sure did care about Sawyer right now.

Sawyer didn't move. "I don't want to go home."

"You can't stay here," she said.

"Why not?"

Confusion kept Sawyer from giving up on his worthless uncle. He had nowhere to go. He only knew he did not want to go home.

"You'll be safe with us," Skylar said.

Julien let her handle the situation.

"Come on. Get your things and let's go."

The boy jumped to his feet in a flash of rage. "You're just going to take me back there!"

"No, we aren't." She glanced at Julien. Could they do that? Just for the night?

"We have to go through the proper channels, but for tonight you're going to stay with me." He glanced at Skylar. "Us."

Her eyes widened a fraction before she covered her reaction.

Sawyer looked at his uncle and then at Julien and Skylar. At last, he walked toward them.

"Your things?" Skylar said.

"They're by the door. My uncle wouldn't let me unpack."

Julien looked back at Conner. "Do you have any kids?"

"Hell no."

"Good." With that, he followed Skylar and the boy out the door.

Back at her house on the ranch, Skylar couldn't believe how her life had taken a sudden left turn. Just days ago she had gone through her everyday routine, enjoying the ranch and occasional outings with friends. She hadn't thought about men or the need for one. She hadn't thought about having children.

She hadn't been shot at, either.

But now, here she was, living with a handsome man and a fourteen-year-old boy who had been exposed to living conditions no child should ever be. She felt out of sorts, like she was living another woman's life, or had supernaturally shifted onto a different course. Where would this lead? Skylar had never not known what direction she would go. She had always been certain ranching and not rushing on getting a man in her life was right for her. And she had always thought a man suited for her would come along naturally.

Julien had come along naturally, but he hadn't seemed suitable. She wondered, then, why she even contemplated such a thing. She had just met him.

Skylar took the pizza from the deliveryman and

brought it to the kitchen. Placing the box on the table, she dished out slices for each of them.

Sawyer had been quiet the whole time. He was clearly not comfortable around strangers and Skylar had the distinct impression he feared being returned to his parents, which pierced her heart.

She and Julien had called Child Protective Services, who had agreed he could stay with them for the night. At least they could give him a night without having to worry about going back to his dysfunctional home.

"Come and get it," she said.

Julien encouraged Sawyer to come to the table. He did, eyes low and avoiding her and Julien.

They ate in silence for a while. When Sawyer finished, he drank several gulps of milk and put down the glass. He eyed first Skylar and then Julien.

"What happens now?" Sawyer asked.

"That depends," Julien said. "I had to report your whereabouts to Child Protective Services. They're going to want to talk to you. Are you okay with that?"

"Do I get to stay here?"

After a moment, Julien said, "They'll be here in the morning to interview you. I told them I didn't think you were safe at your own house."

"Why do they have to talk to me?" Sawyer asked.

"They're going to need to document your living

conditions and environment. Get to know you a little, and what your life is like with your parents."

"What are they going to ask?" Sawyer sounded scared.

"Don't worry," Skylar said. "They care about your safety above all else."

"If they really care, they won't make me go back."

"You should tell the case worker that when they get here," Julien said. "Be honest. Don't make up anything. False accusations are a serious matter." When Sawyer didn't respond, Julien asked, "Do you understand?"

The boy nodded. "I don't have to lie."

Skylar's stomach pitched, dousing her appetite. That did not sound good.

"They'll talk to your parents, too," Julien said. "They'll ask about their financial health, marital problems, substance abuse issues."

"They're gonna lie about all of that."

Skylar feared the boy knew his parents did have those problems.

"CPS will know if they're lying. They deal with people like your parents every day. Your parents will be asked to take drug tests. If they refuse, it will be assumed they are doing drugs."

Sawyer wrung his hands, his head down.

"Don't be afraid," Julien said. "If CPS doesn't protect you, then I will."

Whoa. Skylar heard the strong conviction in Julien's tone, which left no doubt he would do exactly as he said. She felt herself gravitate closer to him spiritually. A man like Julien would not back down, and he would not be afraid.

"My stepfather said he'd…"

Skylar waited for him to go on but he didn't.

"What did your stepfather say?" Julien asked in a calm voice.

After several seconds, Sawyer glanced up at him and then lowered his head again. "If I ever went to the cops he'd…"

"Why does he think you might go to the cops?" Julien asked.

More seconds passed before the boy spoke again. "He…he hits me sometimes."

Julien looked at Skylar and she saw the murderous gleam in his eyes. She almost felt sorry for Sawyer's stepdad. Almost. But she didn't. Anyone who hurt children deserved the worst life could throw at them.

"And…" Sawyer continued, "he tells my mom I lie about it because I don't like him."

"Is that the truth, Sawyer?" Julien asked.

The boy nodded.

"Look me in the eyes and tell me you're telling the truth."

Sawyer looked up and Skylar didn't need to hear any more. Pure torment, and anger, and deep, deep pain consumed his eyes. He was telling the truth and it broke her heart.

"It's okay," Julien said. "I can see you are."

Sawyer lowered his head again and ran his hand over his eyes, no doubt fighting tears. "Is it all right if I go to my room?"

"Of course." Skylar had shown him to the guest room, where he had put his things.

Sawyer stood and walked away.

She watched him until he disappeared at the stairway, then faced Julien.

"You would make a really great dad," she said.

"It isn't hard to be a good parent if you love them."

"There're different levels of good parenting." Skylar had not been hugged very much as a child and often wondered if that's why she wasn't comfortable when people hugged her. A romantic relationship was different, however.

"Skylar, I don't want him going to a foster home. Moving him around so much will do more damage than has already been done."

"You want to foster him until they find a permanent home for him?" she asked.

He hesitated. "Maybe. I don't know."

Julien wasn't considering adopting the boy himself, was he? How could he make a decision like that when he had just met the boy today? But he was a caring person, with an empathetic heart. That

made sense to her because of the passion he had
for his work, helping victims and bringing justice
to bad people.

"Why don't you sleep on it?" she said. "See how
the interview goes tomorrow?"

He met her eyes for long seconds before nodding. "Yeah. Maybe you're right."

She could see he would spend much of this night
awake and thinking about Sawyer's situation.

Skylar thought she might stay up with him.
Something about Julien made her want to be with
him, to comfort him. More. But she wouldn't go
there now.

The woman from Child Protective Services
was a forty-year-old named Tracy Compton who
didn't smile. Julien had spoken with her prior to
their meeting and explained all Sawyer had said
to him last night. He wanted the boy to have every
advantage out of his interview.

Julien watched Sawyer sit at the kitchen table
and eye the woman warily as she came to sit beside him.

Julien took a seat next to Skylar, across from the
other two. She glanced at him and for a moment
their gazes met and that mysterious spark of attraction hit him. That's how it happened with her. Out
of the blue, sexual chemistry rushed forth.

Tracy and Sawyer chatted about little things

for a while before Tracy asked, "Why did you run away?"

Sawyer lowered his head. "My parents were fighting. I hate it when they fight."

"Yelling? Or was it more than that?"

"Yelling."

Julien began to sense that Sawyer was hesitant to elaborate.

Tracy moved on with her questions. "Do they ever yell at you?"

"Yeah. When I do things wrong."

Julien glanced at Skylar, who met his look with equal bewilderment.

"What kind of things?" Tracy asked.

"Don't do as asked, like clean my room or get home late from school without telling them."

That all sounded normal. Why wasn't he telling Tracy everything?

"Has either of your parents hit you?"

Sawyer's hesitation dragged out longer than previously. "No." He bobbed one of his knees up and down.

Julien knew he was lying. As a PI and a former detective, he had gotten very good at recognizing lies when he heard them.

Tracy asked Sawyer more questions, to which Sawyer answered in a way that painted his family life as normal.

When she'd finished and prepared to leave, the CPS worker signaled Julien to join her at the door.

Out of earshot, she told him, "I'll keep the investigation open based on what you told me, but without any real evidence of abuse or neglect, there isn't much I can do."

"What are you saying? That he has to go back there?"

"I'm afraid so." Tracy looked grim.

"He's lying. You know that."

"Sometimes they do that out of fear of repercussions. He probably doesn't trust anyone to get him out of that house."

"So he's afraid of what his parents will do."

"Most likely." Tracy sighed. "I don't want Sawyer back at that house any more than you do. Get me evidence."

What kind of evidence? A beaten and bleeding boy? He felt like punching a hole in the wall.

Tracy put her hand on his arm. "I'm headed over to his parents' now for their interviews. Maybe something will come up there, like Sawyer's mother confessing. If that doesn't happen, then I'll be back to take him home."

Julien didn't hold much hope of any confession. "I can take him. He was my missing person case."

"All right. Give me a couple of hours and then I will call you."

Julien closed the door and went back into the kitchen. Sawyer looked at him shyly.

Sitting in the chair Tracy had vacated, Julien folded his hands on the table. "Why did you lie, Sawyer?"

"I didn't."

He cocked his head. "Yes, you did. What are you afraid of?"

Sawyer banged his hand on the table, making Skylar flinch. "I'm not afraid!" He stood and marched toward the guest room.

Julien hated seeing a child suffer that way. Sawyer's heated reaction only cemented his belief that there was abuse going on in his house.

"Don't be too hard on yourself," Skylar said. "He's dealing with his situation the best he can."

"I'm not going to let him walk back into that dangerous house."

"What can you do?"

Julien bowed his head. He could set up surveillance, but what good would that do if he couldn't see through walls? He could give him a business card and tell him to call if he needed help. But would he call?

Skylar got up and walked around the table, putting her hand on his shoulder. "Maybe it's best this way. You can't adopt every kid you find in a missing person case."

While she did have a valid point, something

about Sawyer felt different. And he had seen how Skylar responded to the boy. She wasn't as anti-kid as she seemed. She wasn't anti-kid at all. Julien realized her cold family just hadn't exposed her to the power of parental love.

Chapter 5

Skylar walked with Julien and Sawyer to the small ranch house that was in marginal disrepair. Tracy had phoned to ask that they bring the boy there. His slow tread contradicted his interview with the social worker. She couldn't fully comprehend how much his predicament meant to her, much less her deepening emotions for Julien. Nor did she want to. This wasn't a good time. She had too much on her mind already, what with a potential killer having targeted her twice.

The boy stepped up onto the cement porch and Tracy opened the door and ushered him inside.

Stepping into the living room, Skylar waited

near the door with Julien. Sawyer's parents sat on the couch and stood as Sawyer approached them.

His mother crouched before him and took him into an embrace. "We were so worried about you. I'm so glad you're all right." She leaned back and planted a kiss to his forehead.

Her reunion appeared genuine to Skylar, but behind the touching display, Sawyer's dad stood with his hands in his jeans' pockets, a grim line to his mouth.

"I'll be back to check on you," Tracy said to the trio.

Sawyer's mother looked up at Julien. "Thank you for finding him."

Julien gave her a nod of acknowledgment.

Then she looked at Skylar. "And for taking care of him."

"Of course," Skylar said.

Julien turned his gaze to Sawyer's dad. There was no mistaking the warning in his eyes.

Tracy walked to the door and said to Julien, "There's nothing else we can do here. Let's step outside."

Skylar took Julien's hand and gently urged him out the door before he did something rash. They walked behind Tracy toward their cars.

Tracy stopped and faced them. "As you can see, nothing of significance came up in the interview. I spoke with them separately and then together. John

Larkin didn't say much. He gave one-word answers and had a brooding look about him the entire time. He let his wife answer all the financial questions during the couple's interview."

Julien pinched the bridge of his nose.

"Melissa seemed nervous, but honest," Tracy said. "She didn't appear to have been coached prior to the interview. When I told her the things Sawyer said to you, Julien, she didn't believe it. She said her son made that up because he doesn't like John."

"What about bruises?" Julien asked. "Did you ask her if she ever saw any?"

"Yes, and she said Sawyer told her they were the result of fights at school."

"Sawyer told her that?" Julien said dubiously.

"Most likely Sawyer was threatened to say that." Julien muttered a curse.

"Don't worry," Tracy said. "I will be visiting regularly and I'll be looking for anything suspicious."

"Thank you for trying," Skylar said.

Tracy gave a nod and turned to go.

Skylar caught sight of the front window of the ranch house and spotted John standing in the window. He was watching them like some spectral being. The man made her skin crawl. To think Sawyer had to live with him made her heart sink. It also shocked her, because she had a feeling her deep concern would surely involve her as much as Julien.

She shook her head. Ever since she had met him,

her life wasn't the same. She'd discovered things about herself she had no idea existed.

Looking at Julien, she saw him observing her. Grimness still surrounded his eyes, but he seemed to regard her with solemn curiosity. A fleeting thought of how it would be to have kids with him gave her a jolt. She didn't know this woman who was emerging. Julien—a handsome, strong, righteous man—stimulated that growth. He appealed to her on so many levels when he shouldn't. Or had she been wrong about that?

On the way back to Skylar's, her phone rang and Julien was glad for the distraction. He didn't want to analyze how much Sawyer affected him. Or how Skylar's increasing affinity for the boy affected him, too. He sensed her struggle with the change herself. Maybe she was kid material, after all. Dare he hope?

"My brother Corbin is up at the main house. I need to go talk to him."

Julien didn't ask why. "I'll go with you." He hadn't let her out of his sight since he'd come here and he wasn't about to now. He'd been sidetracked by the missing person case and finding Sawyer, but her predicament had never left his mind and he'd been vigilant.

Nearly back at the ranch anyway, they arrived in just a few minutes.

Julien entered Skylar's parents' large home behind her and heard voices in the kitchen. As they appeared, Skylar's mother—Francesca, he remembered—looked up from the table, a teacup in front of her. Julien presumed the man across from her was Skylar's brother. He bore a striking resemblance to Cal with his dark hair and light blue eyes.

"Mom said you were having a meltdown," Skylar said.

"Hello, Julien," her mother said.

"Ma'am."

"Ambrosia's divorcing me," her brother said. "Everything was going fine until one day I came home from work and she had all my clothes packed. *My clothes,* not hers. She said she didn't love me and never had. All very coldhearted, blurting it out like our marriage or I didn't matter. She then proceeded to inform me that she wanted the house and the Mercedes, half my retirement and alimony." Corbin shook his head and ran his hand through his hair.

"What did you think you were getting into when you married her?" Skylar asked. "She isn't exactly a hometown girl. She's materialistic and shallow. But all you saw was her looks. Correct me if I'm wrong."

He just stared at her.

"Let me guess," Skylar continued. "Was she

married before you? Was the guy wealthy? Has she ever worked a day in her life?"

He lowered his gaze. "Her first husband was a lawyer. And I don't think she ever had to work."

"There you go." Skylar lifted her hand in an aha gesture. "You can't keep picking that kind of woman, Corbin. You won't find true love that way."

Corbin glanced at Julien, who continued to stay out of this brother-sister talk. But he felt for the guy. Julien knew what it was like to strike out in love.

"I thought I had that with Ambrosia. She really threw me when she asked me to leave."

"I'm surprised, too," Francesca said, sipping some tea. "She's quite beautiful, and I never had any trouble with her."

Julien saw no resemblance between Skylar and her mother, other than some physical features. Clearly the woman couldn't see what made for a good person.

"I always knew it was a matter of time." Skylar went to the table and took the seat beside Corbin. "Never mind that. I don't mean to be insulting, but I warned you when you announced you were going to marry her."

"You didn't know her," Corbin said.

"You can do so much better, Corbin. Is it going to take losing half of everything you have to learn that?"

"Skylar, don't start that again," Corbin said.

She placed her hand atop his. "All I'm saying is that you have a second chance to find someone genuine. Don't settle for the gold diggers."

That must have been why Skylar had come here, to impress upon her brother not to make the same mistake in the future, Julien thought.

"Skylar does have a point, Corbin," Francesca said. "If you keep ending up with women who divorce you for money, you'll end up poor."

Corbin didn't say anything, just lowered his head and stared at his cooling cup of tea.

Julien watched Skylar observe her brother with a mixture of sympathy and disappointment. She cared about her family, which Julien found interesting given all Cal had told him, and Skylar herself, for that matter.

"Have you told your father yet?" Francesca asked.

"No."

"He's going to blow up," Skylar said.

"He'll also find you an excellent lawyer," Francesca added.

Abruptly, Corbin stood. "I shouldn't have come here."

Skylar started after him but Francesca stopped her. "Leave him alone, Skylar."

Skylar faced her mother, concern and anguish etched in her face. Julien had a feeling something else had to be fueling her emotion. The way she had rushed to her brother's side and the passion she'd showed over his situation, suggested a more personal motive. Julien had a hunch that she had been burned in a similar way.

"He'll be all right and he won't make the same mistake," Francesca said. "He's a lot like your father that way. He can't stand being made to feel like a fool."

Sitting back down, Skylar fell into thought, looking away and out the patio window. Julien took the seat Corbin had vacated. Skylar didn't turn from the window, so engrossed in whatever plagued her. He became transfixed by her profile, her sloping nose, those long eyelashes and stunning blue eyes so filled with somberness. He almost reached over and put his hand on hers.

"Cal leaves and I see you more than ever, Julien," Francesca said, diverting his attention.

Seeing her changed expression, he knew she had been observing him keenly just now.

"You're spending a lot of time with my daughter."

That brought Skylar out of her melancholic stare.

"She's been attacked. I don't want her to be alone," he said, thinking that ought to be plenty of an explanation.

"Yes, I do see the need for that, but you two must be getting to know each other," Francesca said.

"Mother..." Skylar protested.

"I'm just curious, that's all. You haven't dated anyone in a long time. You're long overdue. And I'd like more than Cal to be working on giving me grandchildren."

"Mother, please. Since when do you care about my personal life?" Skylar snapped, sounding defensive, which told Julien her mother had struck a nerve.

"I've always cared, and you watch your tone with me."

Skylar averted her head, once again taking refuge in the view through the patio window.

"Have you found the man who shot at my daughter?" Francesca asked Julien.

"No, unfortunately, I had a missing person case I needed to wrap up. Now that that's out of the way, I can focus more."

"There's talk that Wes McKann is a suspect."

"He's a person of interest," Julien said. Wes did look guilty but, in Julien's line of work, he had learned wait for the evidence.

"No one likes him. He's so grouchy all the time, and a lone wolf. If he didn't kill his wife, then Charlotte must have finally left him. We all thought she should have left years ago. They never had any children. From what I hear, Wes works the ranch from dawn until dusk. That can't have been good on their relationship."

"You're getting interested in gossip as you age,

Mom," Skylar said. "You used to prefer people talk about you, how fortunate you are."

"I still enjoy that attention." Francesca laughed lightly. "I don't deny it. I love your father, but I wouldn't have married him if he hadn't had a lot of money. There's security in money."

"Up until an apocalypse, I suppose," Skylar quipped.

"Even then." Her mother waved her hand dismissively.

"There's also a lawyer's wife who is missing. I'm looking into both cases." Julien didn't say he had a hunch the alleged body Skylar had seen was one of those women.

"Who's the lawyer?" Francesca asked.

"Benson Davett," Julien said.

"Aren't the police investigating that and Wes's wife's disappearance?"

"Yes, but I'm doing my own private investigation."

"I've heard of Ben Davett. I've seen him and his wife at a lot of the same social events Newman and I attend. He's a corporate attorney. Audrey is a lovely woman. Very beautiful and poised. She was in her element at the most prestigious gatherings. I can't imagine he'd do anything to harm his wife. Is he the one who called the police?"

Julien really couldn't imagine a man like Davett hurting his wife, either. Benson had called the police the night Audrey hadn't come home. He had said it wasn't like her to be gone all day, much less not be home in the evening unless they had something planned, like a dinner party. She had gone shopping earlier in the day and wasn't there when Benson had arrived home from work. He also said she hadn't answered her phone the two times he had tried.

"Yes, he did," he told Skylar's mother.

Francesca pointed her finger and bounced it up and down a couple of times. "Now, that Wes character? I can completely imagine him harming his wife."

"So can I." Skylar pulled her phone from her back pocket when it dinged with an incoming text. "I need to get to work." She got up, went around the table. "Bye, Mom."

"See you soon, Sky."

Julien caught her smile and speculative look she aimed at them.

Once outside, Julien couldn't wait any longer to ask Skyler the question that had been echoing in his mind. "I think there's more to your avoiding having a family of your own. Am I right?"

She snapped a quick glance his way and stopped at the driver's door of her truck. "What brought that on?"

"The way you got on your bother about his choice in women."

"He has bad taste."

Julien didn't know Ambrosia, but he, personally, would know if a woman didn't have feelings for him. Maybe that didn't matter to Corbin. His passion was business.

"Yes, but you went over the top on him," he said.

She looked off to her left, where the rolling landscape was bathed in sunlight. Then, responding to his previous comment, returned defensive eyes to him, saying, "I wouldn't say I *avoid*."

He smiled. "Okay, 'not consider it.'"

Her head cocked slightly and she turned to him. "What makes you say that?"

"The level of worry you had in there, rushing over as soon as you heard he was having a problem, and then that heartfelt conversation. I mean, I get that he's your brother, but I had the sense that you had a personal investment."

After several seconds just looking at him, she nodded her head. "Yes, something like that did happen to me. It was a man who worked for my father as a manager. When I first met him, I didn't know he had his sights on a VP position and even a chief position. He was looking for a fast track and must have decided I would do."

Julien put his hand on the door frame, part of him desiring to be closer to her. "Quite the charmer, huh?"

She looked over at his arm and then back to his face, her eyes considerably more aware of him.

"Yes, Bryce was definitely that. We were together a few months when he told me he had feelings for me and thought we made a good couple. I agreed because we did get along and he was always so nice and funny and intelligent. I thought I had feelings for him, too. I certainly hadn't felt that way with anyone else before. When he proposed, I was taken aback, but I said yes."

Wow. She had nearly gotten married? Julien didn't understand the flash of jealousy he experienced just then.

"But when he said he wanted to get married in a month, I began to question why. Why the big rush? I told him we should wait. He let it drop that night but he kept bringing it up." She fell silent and he could tell she had felt significant betrayal over her discovery of the guy's true motives.

"How did you find out?" he asked. And what, exactly.

Skylar seemed reluctant to talk in any detail. "Let's go."

Disappointed and more curious than ever, Julien let her get in and went to sit on the passenger seat.

After she drove a while, he asked, "Are you going to leave me in suspense?"

She glanced over and surprised him with a slight smile. "I don't like talking about it."

"I don't like talking about my past relationships, either." But after this, he was sure that was coming.

Skylar bit her lower lip. "I heard Bryce talking with his mother. She asked him if he was sure he wanted to go through with the marriage and he answered yes, that he wasn't in love with me but he liked me enough. He said, 'I can move up in the company faster and, with all the money those Chelseys have, I can take care of you so much better.'" She sighed. "I will never forget hearing that—the sound of his voice, the words. He didn't sound the same as when he spoke with me. I realized the man I had agreed to marry wasn't the one he had been presenting to me all those months."

Clearly upset recalling the memory, Skylar turned her eyes toward the window and then back to the windshield.

He had to ask. "What did you do?"

"After I heard him?" Skylar sighed again. "I left without saying goodbye."

That sounded like something she would do, with all her spunk.

"I didn't answer his calls or answer my door. I told my father what he'd said and my father fired him. That's how Bryce found out I was on to him. He stalked me for a while, but stopped after my father sent someone to deliver him a message." She glanced over at him. "Bryce wasn't hurt much, just sufficiently threatened."

Julien whistled. "Don't mess with the Chelsey offspring."

"He was told we would go to the police if he didn't stop stalking me."

And what else had been done to him? She said he hadn't been "hurt much." That might be something. If anyone had stalked *his* sister, he probably would have done the same.

"Did the two of you talk about having a family?" he asked.

Her fists tightened on the wheel and one of them ground a little. "I know why you're asking."

"I would be disappointed if you didn't." He was enormously amused and unwillingly drawn to her as a person—as a woman.

"We did," she said at last.

He waited. And waited. Waited some more.

"He asked me if I wanted children," she finally said.

Julien did not comment. He did not have to be told Bryce had asked and she had said no, making her the perfect candidate for his endeavor of securing wealth without earning it on his own.

"Have you been with anyone since Bryce?" He couldn't be sure if she had or not and didn't really know why that was important to him.

She wrung her hand on the wheel. "Enough about me."

Why was it so difficult for her to talk about her love life? Had she been betrayed more than once?

"You don't trust anyone, is that it?" he asked, hoping to help her out.

"I would like to find a man not out to take advantage of me," she said, "but I don't waste my time trying."

She wrung her hands on the wheel again. "Why are you asking anyway? What about you? You haven't mentioned anything about your past relationships."

So, love was a touchy subject? Skylar had already alluded that she hadn't dated much due to work anyway, so he didn't push her. "I came close to marriage once. Similar to your experience, she ended up being someone different than she presented." Thinking of Renee, her duplicity stung with its usual potency, but luckily, over the last few years, Julien had thought of her less and less. He hadn't thought of her at all since meeting Skylar.

When they arrived at the ranch, Skylar came to a stop in front of her house and turned to look at him. "What did she do?"

"It's not so much what she did as what she said." He remembered when he'd first met Renee. It had been so natural and unplanned. "I went to a baseball game with another P.I. and she was sitting next to me with her friend. We hit it off and started dating. She owned an art gallery. I found her earthy and real."

"When really she was worldly and fake?" Skylar said with a wry smile.

"Yes. Or, more plainly, a liar. Turns out, she had a fantasy of being with one of the infamous Dark Alley Investigators. She couldn't have Kadin, so she took whatever she could get her hands on."

"You, I take it."

He chuckled. "Yeah, until I found out she was sleeping with my friend Joe, the one who went to the game with me."

Skylar inhaled sharply. "You lost both her and your friend."

"That's when she told me about her fantasy and how Joe made her realize she was fooling herself."

She met his eyes and he could feel her empathy. "Well," she said at last, "we're both in professions that consume large quantities of our time and we've had our hearts ripped out by people who wanted us for something other than love."

"Everything in common but our addresses." He chuckled.

She laughed lightly and they passed a few minutes in silence. Finally, she turned to him. "I still have to go out and check the fence. I never did get the chance to finish that job." She didn't have to tell him why. Neither of them had forgotten the body and the gunman she'd encountered on her last venture out there.

"I'll go with you. Can we drive?"

"Absolutely not."

Chapter 6

With everyone hard at work in various parts of the ranch, Skylar saddled up Bogie and a gentle spirited brown quarter horse named Willow. Julien leaned against a stall door, one leg bent and the holster of his gun peeking out from his spring jacket. He looked like he could be on the cover of *Horse and Rancher* magazine. Be still her beating heart…

Leading the two horses from the stable, she took them outside the corral and handed him Willow's reins. He stood there motionless as she mounted Bogie, not bothering to hide how closely he watched her.

Putting his foot—thankfully he had on boots—

into the stirrup, he drew a little momentum by bouncing up and down a couple times, then propelled himself onto the horse. He adjusted the reins.

"You look like you've ridden before," she said, meaning it.

He sent her an unappreciative glance.

Smiling, Skylar guided Bogie toward the pastures. Willow would follow. She and Bogie had a thing for each other.

Riding side-by-side, Skylar took in the beauty of the rolling hills and the cluster of trees flanking the river, too aware of Julien. He sat atop the horse straight and tall, sunglasses hiding his eyes, wisps of blond hair fluttering in a soft breeze. His head turned and he caught her glance. They shared a long look before Skylar faced forward again.

Then she saw him scanning their surroundings and knew he had not stopped being vigilant. She felt safer and more at ease with going out riding. Still, she glanced around herself, eerily reminded of her frantic run from flying bullets.

Many parts of the ranch held memories of her youth but this was one of her favorites. She had loved riding here, along the river and fence line. She hadn't thought of this before, but she had a lot of good memories of growing up. Not just out here, on horseback, but at home, as well.

But her good mood didn't last long. Once they came upon the area where she had seen the man digging, she sobered. She felt her stomach tense as they rode closer. Memories bombarded her. Who was the person wrapped in plastic? She was certain it had been a body. She stopped Bogie and stared, feeling her skin crawl as she imagined someone had been killed. And she envisioned the gun aimed at her.

Julien drew his horse up beside hers. "There's nobody here now, Skylar. I'm watching." It was as if he'd read her mind again. "I'd like to go question some of the workers at Wes's ranch. You're going to have to come with me," he said.

For her protection, he meant. "All right. Let me get some work done today and we can go tomorrow."

They resumed their ride, checking the fence as they crested a hill and headed down the other side. The sound of a rattle preceded Julien's horse rearing up with a whinny.

Rattlesnake.

Julien lost his seat and the horse galloped off in the direction of the stable.

Seeing Julien on his back, Skylar dismounted and went to him, searching for the snake and not seeing the culprit. It must have slithered off.

"Are you all right?" She knelt beside him and leaned over his face.

"Yeah. My butt might be bruised." He sat up.

She looked around for the snake again and then turned back to him. "You'll get used to it."

"Why do I doubt that?" he said. "I don't know how you do this."

Skylar was still shaken up over the snake. She had not seen one on the ranch in years. Had someone put it there on purpose? She didn't see how—or why. How would the shooter have known they would be out here?

"What's wrong?" Julien asked.

Skylar shook her head briefly. She must just be easily spooked these days. "I guess I keep expecting someone to jump out and try to kill me."

"That's why I'm here."

She smiled a little, grateful for his effort to ease her mind.

He met her eyes and responded with a soft smile, as well. A spark passed between them, creating a new tension.

"How often do you ride?" he asked.

Again, he had a way of alleviating fear.

"Every day." She sat on her rear as he leaned back and propped himself up on his elbows.

"On purpose?"

She laughed again. "I love riding. Why not work and ride if I can?"

"You'll have to give me a horse that doesn't spook so easily," he said.

"Willow is the calmest horse we have. She just doesn't like snakes."

"Must be my lucky day then."

She enjoyed his good-sporting humor. She enjoyed his smiling eyes even more. But as he noticed her attention, she saw the subtle change to his face. His eyes lowered to her mouth and slowly went back up to her eyes, where he captured her gaze. The moment warmed, as it often did with him, this ineffable spark. She allowed herself the luxury of doing the same to him, sinking into the pleasure of absorbing his handsome face, those blue eyes that she could stare at for hours, those full lips she imagined kissing.

Sitting straighter, Julien slipped his left hand behind her head and made her imagination come to life as his lips pressed to hers. Fiery sensation quickly intensified. She had to catch her breath, opening her mouth to get more air and, in the process, inviting him in for a deeper melding. She put one hand on his chest and slid her other over his shoulder to the back of his neck, her fingers in his hair.

Powerful sexual need boiled to an unbearable level. Skylar's surroundings dropped away and all she could focus on was Julien and his stimulating kiss. Was he just a good kisser or was this her natural response to him? She feared it was the latter.

Bogie nudged her on her back with his soft nose,

breaking them apart. She looked into Julien's smoldering eyes, knowing he felt as bewildered as she did. Bogie gave her another nudge, pushing her toward Julien.

Laughing, she looked up as the horse put his head over her shoulder and smelled Julien, blowing air and nickering.

"I think he approves," Skylar said, rubbing Bogie's cheek.

Julien didn't share her humor. He still stared at her, barely acknowledging the gelding.

Skylar got to her feet and, after a brief delay, Julien did the same. He said nothing as she mounted the horse, removing her foot from the stirrup so he could get up behind her. Once seated, he slid his hand around her stomach, slow and seductive, and then the other.

The same heat that had roared forth with the kiss inundated her now. Bogie's smooth walk and the clear day added to the allure of the man behind her. She lifted her head and turned to him.

Leaving one hand on her stomach, Julien placed the palm of his other on her cheek and lowered his head until their lips met. At first, light and slow, the kiss didn't take long to grow into insatiable hunger. Skylar held the reins in one hand and put her other on his thigh, needing to have some contact with him—more contact. He slid his hand from her cheek to her breast. Feeling her, caressing her.

She was on fire for him.

He lifted his head and she opened her eyes to the answering inferno in his. She breathed heavy and felt flushed.

Hearing voices, Skylar faced forward and saw that they'd reached the outbuildings of the ranch. Shawn, her deputy ranch manager, was flogging a horse inside the round pen and her best groom, Marko, was yelling at him to stop. He stood outside the training pen, holding Willow's reins.

Skylar urged Bogie into a gallop, hoping Julien wouldn't fall off again. He didn't.

As she slowed Bogie to a stop in front of the training pen, Shawn lowered the crop he had used as a whip. The young black horse's eyes were wide with fear.

"Get away from him," Skylar ordered as Julien dismounted.

Shawn did so with lowered eyebrows.

Skylar jumped down from Bogie's back and marched over to the fence. "Get out of there." She was so angry she nearly laid into Shawn with a diatribe of reproach.

Shawn walked slowly toward the gate, which Marko opened for him with a glare.

"Nobody beats my animals," she said.

"That horse is headstrong. It needs to be shown who's in charge," Shawn retorted belligerently.

This wasn't the first time he'd argued with her.

He had a problem with her being his boss. He always had. She couldn't figure out if he simply had issues with authority or if he didn't like taking orders from a woman.

"We don't train our horses that way," Skylar said.

"He beats all the animals," Marko said.

Shawn rounded on him. "You're a liar. Stay out of this or I'll fire you."

The groom shut his mouth and continued to glare at Shawn.

"You won't be firing anyone," Skylar said. Then, to Marko, she asked, "Is that true? All the animals?"

"Maybe not all, but I've seen him use that crop on other horses at least three other times."

"This ranch needs to be run by someone with a backbone," Shawn said, clearly getting angrier by the second.

"It also needs to be run by someone with humanity," Skylar said.

"Is that something you think you have?" Shawn asked.

Skylar couldn't believe the way he spoke to her. Apparently, he had taken all he could of working for a woman.

"You had all of this handed to you," he raged at her, "including your position as ranch manager. You never worked for any of it. Me? I worked my ass off to get where I was before you decided to take my job. I started mucking stalls when I was fifteen. It took me ten years to get to ranch manager."

Insulted beyond measure, Skylar said, "How dare you say I didn't work for what I have. I've worked on this ranch since I was a little girl. I mucked stalls long before my fifteenth birthday, so I don't understand your point."

Shawn began to simmer down. She could see in his eyes that he realized he had gone too far. Regardless, she had no choice.

"I can't have someone with your temperament working here. You're fired, Shawn. Get your things and leave."

The anger fled completely from his eyes. "What? Just like that? Look, I admit to losing my patience at times, but firing me is a bit extreme. I'll leave training to someone else from now on. You don't have to fire me."

Skylar could see it took all of his self-discipline to grind out those duteous words. "No, I think I do."

Once again, a violent storm crowded his brow and he stepped closer, towering over her, his height nearly at Julien's. "You can't fire me. You can't run this place without me."

Julien moved forward, his pistol in the side holster plainly visible.

Shawn glanced his way, saw the pistol and met Skylar's eyes with more hostility.

"Get off my ranch," Skylar said. "Now."

With one more look at Julien, Shawn turned and walked to his truck.

"Marko," Skylar said, "would you go get two or three of the biggest cattle cowboys and ask them to wait outside Shawn's house to make sure he leaves?"

"Yes, ma'am." Marko didn't move. "There's something else you should know."

Skylar became thoroughly attentive. What else would he bring to light?

"Shawn's girlfriend didn't come home last night."

Shawn had a girlfriend?

"How do you know that?"

"She moved in with him a few weeks ago. I heard them fighting. Thing is, I haven't heard fighting in a while. When I asked him where she was, he said he didn't know."

A chill rode up her spine. She had the distinct impression that Marko was implying something he wasn't exactly saying. And then it hit her. Did Marko think Shawn's girlfriend could be the body she had seen wrapped in plastic? Recalling that Shawn had left just after she had spoken to him that day, she wondered if it was possible he had driven to the spot where she had seen the gunman. He had about the right build. The vehicle was different than the one he drove, though he could have parked his somewhere else.

Julien stepped forward. "Why didn't you say something sooner?"

"I didn't know until yesterday. Jessica—one of the other grooms—said Felicia told her she was afraid of Shawn. He'd threatened her that if she left him, he would kill her."

His words hit like a big bomb dropping out of the sky. Skylar glanced at Julien.

"What's Felicia's last name?" he asked.

"Monroe?" Marko thought a few seconds longer. "No, Montague."

"Do you know anything else about her? Family? Friends? Where she lived prior to this?"

Marko shook his head. "Not really. She had a Southern accent and I know she worked as a waitress in Waldon."

Waldon was a small town north of Irving, not far from the ranch.

"What restaurant?" Julien asked.

"I think she said Maxine's."

Skylar had been there a few times. It was a cute little café.

"I don't know her," Marko said. "I just thought it was suspicious, with Skylar seeing that body and all."

"Thank you, Marko. I'll check into it," Julien said.

As Marko went off to find some big cowboys to escort her ex-deputy ranch manager off the property, Skylar's mind whirred. Shawn lived rent-free in one of three fully furnished houses on the property. He had it made here. Why would he risk ruining that with this blowup? More important, had he killed his girlfriend?

"What do you make of that?" she asked Julien.

"Could he have made it to that area of fence line?" he asked.

"Yes. He had ample time. But he knew I was going to check the fence. Why would he risk being seen?"

"Did you ride the fence line right away?"

"No. I checked on some cattle first." She paused a second and then added, "And I told him I would."

"So, he could have thought he had time."

She still thought it would be too risky. Shawn was many things, but stupid wasn't one of them. Still, Skylar felt glad she had fired him. But could she be sure he wouldn't come back?

Julien insisted they go into Irving tonight. His main motive for taking her was to get Skylar's mind off dead bodies and ranch workers who might be responsible for murder. His ulterior motive was to be somewhere public after those explosive kisses. But now he seriously questioned his logic.

The driver he had arranged to take them opened the back door of the dark sedan in front of the restaurant. Julien got out first and then the vision that had arrested his senses when he'd first seen her emerge from her stairway stepped out.

One knee peeked from the waist-high slit in the silky black dress. Transparent lace covered the gap in the slit to her ankles, making it a teasingly sexy getup. As she unfolded her body from inside the car, she unwittingly gave him a birds-eye view of the dipping neckline. Her breasts were not too small or too large. They were made for his hands and mouth.

He offered his hand and walked with her to the entrance of the restaurant, one worthy of her family name and of him. Stepping into Edward's Prime Seafood, he appreciated the soft lighting that set the right mood.

The hostess took them to their table.

"You know, I have been to restaurants before," Skylar said as she sat.

He went to his chair. "Yes, but not with me."

She smiled, her face lightly made up and her hair in a sophisticated updo, tendrils falling on each side of her face.

"Is this supposed to make me yearn for the city?" she asked.

"Maybe not yearn, but visit more often." In truth, he did secretly hope to sway her away from her ranch lifestyle. Any woman who revved his engine the way she did with just a kiss was worth pursuing.

Part of him warned he should be careful. Skylar was not an uncertain woman. She would not make big decisions haphazardly. He could wind up falling for her only to end up losing her.

"What, exactly, do you like about the city?" she asked after they ordered something from the bar.

"Everything. The noise. Lots of people. Things to do."

"The crime?"

"I wouldn't say I *like* crime. I like solving it. What is it about ranching you like so much?"

"The opposite of what appeals to you about the city. The quiet. No people. As far as things to do, I can always drive to the city if the urge ever strikes."

Meaning she rarely had the urge.

"Surely you get tired of doing the same thing every day. Don't you ever want to catch a movie or a play or a concert or go somewhere like a museum or amusement park? Maybe a festival or two?"

"Oh, I *love* festivals. But they usually involve hay and horses. You can't tell me that a good old-fashioned Western festival doesn't tempt you at all," she said.

No, actually it did have its fair share of pull. "I would enjoy that. We went to a lot of them when I was growing up on the farm. I usually don't miss the State Fair, either."

Her head tipped slightly to one side in fascination. "Really?"

"Believe it or not, yes. I like the rides and the music, and of course, the food trucks."

"Maybe you're not as much of a city man as you think you are."

"Maybe you're not as much of a cowgirl as you think you are."

He met her eyes and could feel her thinking they could not ignore their differences. Maybe they weren't so different, but choosing a place to live was significant.

Their wine arrived and they paused their conversation to savor it. Then Skylar met his eyes and spoke. "Can I ask you something really personal?"

If she had to ask his permission, it must be something big. "Sure."

"Why did you really join Dark Alley Investigations?"

There were numerous reasons he's signed on with DAI. Its mission was to go above and beyond to find justice for victims and their families. Investigators had the freedom to work a case without reporting to anyone. The only rule was to preserve evidence.

But his real reason for joining them? Well, he never talked about it. It still felt so fresh. He looked at her and he saw the genuine curiosity in her eyes. "My uncle Redford was murdered."

He hoped she wouldn't question him too much.

"Oh, I'm so sorry," she said. "When did that happen, and how?"

Julien had been close to his uncle. They'd fished

and camped every year. He and Cal had talked about him when Cal had told him about his grandfather's death. Memories of his uncle still carried angry pain.

"He died when I was with the Rangers. He'd always been healthy, never ill. He should have lived until he was a hundred. But after he lost his wife, he married again. Evelyn—"

"Wait…you think his wife killed him?" Skylar asked.

"Evelyn is many things, but warm or loving isn't one of them. In my opinion, she's more than capable of killing. She was coldhearted and self-centered." He had never sensed any true love for his uncle, either, nor any sign of emotional attachment to anyone, not even to her kids. She had a snake's charm and Julien had never believed most of what she'd said. She was apathetic. Narcissistic. Manipulative and superficial. All the things that characterized a psychopath.

"How did he die?" Skylar asked.

"Pulmonary fibrosis. It took more than a year," Julien said. "People die naturally from that, of course, but because of Evelyn's evil nature, I looked into poisons. Paraquat is an herbicide that, for one thing, if ingested, can cause pulmonary fibrosis. Most victims die within weeks but the timing depends greatly on the dose. I found one case where the victim ingested a small amount and survived, but died months later of pulmonary fibrosis."

"The doctors weren't suspicious about your uncle's death?"

"No. Evelyn even took him to the Mayo Clinic, as if she truly meant to help him. The only thing she ever did was help him into his urn." He looked down into his wine, hating having to relive the memories. "When she had him cremated, there was no possibility for tissue samples, even though the poison had long since left his system. But I started looking into her background and found out her first husband died in a similar fashion. He was also cremated."

Skylar sat back, staring at him in amazement. "How long was she married to her husbands?"

"Ten years to her first. Fifteen to my uncle."

"Why would she murder them after being married to them so long?"

"She enjoyed their money while they were alive. Once it was gone, she forced Red to take out several life insurance policies. Combined, they were worth one and a half million."

"That's a solid motive." Skylar sat in silence for a moment. "Did your uncle love her?"

"He didn't want to be alone after his wife died," Julien said. "No, I don't think he loved her. Not the way he loved Luna."

Julien knew Redford was never the same after

his wife died. He was vulnerable when he met Evelyn. She filled a void and that's all, he thought.

"Where is she now?" Skylar asked.

Julien didn't like thinking about Evelyn walking around alive and spending all that money. "She sold their house in Idaho and moved to Texas to be closer to her kids. No doubt so they could take care of her in her old age," he said.

Skylar leaned forward and placed her hand over his on the table. "Losing your uncle that way must have been so hard."

"What I find the most disturbing is that, in my heart, I just know she killed him, but I have no evidence."

"You couldn't get an autopsy?" Sitting back again, Skylar's eyes widened with shock and fascination.

"I could have forced them to do one, but the doctors said an autopsy wouldn't produce any conclusive evidence." He blew out a frustrated breath. "Trust me, if I thought there was the slightest chance of sending her off to prison to rot where she belongs, I'd have made sure she was charged with murder."

"That, I believe," Skylar said. "You are not the giving up type."

"That's the only murder case I was never able to solve." And that was what bothered him the most—that he hadn't been able to solve it and that his uncle was the victim. "That's why I'm still here," he told her, reaching out for her hand. "Because I won't give up until I find the guy who shot at you."

Chapter 7

Skylar took Julien's hand as he helped her into the Italian Gondola. He'd surprised her by walking her over to the Mandalay Canals after dinner. She sat on the bench and he sat next to her, putting his arm around her, while a man rowed behind them.

"This canal was inspired by the canals in Venice," he said.

She took in the stone arches of a building they passed and the streetlights shining on a few people walking in front of a closed shop and a dimly lit restaurant. Terra cotta roofs slanted down, and they floated beneath a stone bridge.

"It's beautiful."

"Yes. It's one of my favorite things in the city," he said.

"You're a romantic?" He didn't strike her as the type. He seemed too manly for that. But then, she supposed even the most manly of men could be romantic when he wanted a woman. Did Julien want her?

"Just showing you Irving."

The idea of him wanting her flirted with her heartstrings. "I've been to Irving a lot." She knew the city well. "I do like the city, Julien. I just don't want to live in it."

He said nothing and faced forward, looking at another approaching stone bridge.

"You do realize I'm going have to take you on a hayride now," she said, teasing him. She didn't want to ruin this perfect evening with him, and dared to call it a date. It was a date, wasn't it? He hadn't actually asked her on one. He had only said he was taking her to dinner in Irving.

He chuckled. "I look forward to it."

Ever since she'd learned they had different predilections about places to live, she had been thinking more and more about how she'd given up her dream of interior design. She did love the ranch and the animals, but she had never given interior design a chance. How could she say that career wouldn't give her the same passion as ranching?

She imagined designing a client's house, maybe

an old Victorian, and her mind raced with colors and textures and furnishings. She felt good, as she always did when she made changes in her own house.

The boat floated by an upscale restaurant where a couple sat at a small round patio table, holding hands beside a glowing candle. Skylar felt warm and relaxed. The ambience couldn't be better, especially with a man like Julien, who had clearly put a lot of thought and planning into this evening. She had never met a man who treated her this special.

Skylar adjusted her body to fit closer to Julien's, snuggled in the curve of his arm. She rested her head on his shoulder and gave in to the lights of the shops and businesses that lined the canal.

Julien's hand caressed her arm, automatic and purely innocent. She closed her eyes to the sweetness.

When she opened her eyes and looked up, she saw Julien's face so close to hers. His eyes were warm with…not passion, but relaxed chemistry. She could think of no other way to describe the exchange. They had a fiery connection but, right now, just being together felt good. So right. She had never felt this way with any other man.

Disconcerted, she moved her head and looked up at the stars, clearer now that the gondola had floated away from the brighter building lights.

By the time the gondolier steered over to the

side of the canal, indicating to Skylar that the tour was over, she was relieved. She needed some space from Julien, from this growing intimacy. Overly conscious of her sexy dress—one she had chosen for this *date*—she stepped onto the dock. Julien tipped the gondolier and put his hand on her lower back as he guided her to the street.

Seeing the sleek sedan and a driver waiting, she wondered how Julien could afford all of this—the elegant dinner, the gondola ride, the rented car.

Julien opened the back door for her and she slid inside, settling on the back seat to wait for him to reach the other side and get in.

Skylar doubted even a prestigious private investigation agency like Dark Alley would provide a sedan for a personal night out.

"What made you arrange for all of this, Julien?" she asked.

"I wanted us to have a special night."

"But…why?" She really needed to know. Was he interested in her or was he trying to find out how viable they were as a couple?

"To provide an escape from bodies wrapped in plastic and the threat of another attack or house invasion," he said.

Hoping to hide her disappointment, she turned away and watched the streetlights pass.

"And because I wanted to spend some time with you like this," he added. "Because I like you."

Turning back to him, she felt butterflies tickle her abdomen. "Then you are as curious as I am. And this is a date, isn't it?"

"Sure. I wanted to see what this thing is between us. When I kissed you, it made a big impact."

Skylar felt the same. Although she also wondered if there was anything to them as a couple, she wasn't sure they should delve into it too much. "You didn't have to go to all this trouble just for that."

"If you're worried about the money I spent on tonight, don't. I have money. My parents set up trust funds for me and my sister. They made a fortune on their flower seed farm. We're set for life."

Skylar lost her breath. She stared into Julien's blue eyes, struggling with her passionate reaction to him as a man and the meaning of what he had just said. She couldn't process how his words threw her off kilter.

He had money. He wasn't anything like Bryce or the other men like him who had used her to get to her wealth.

"So, now you know I'm not after you for your money," he said.

Her body flushed with sexual need. He triggered a primal reaction in her. "I hate that you felt you had to tell me that. I hate even more that it makes me feel safer with you."

He chuckled. "The night isn't over yet."

What did he mean by that? She glanced around,

seeing where the sedan was headed. Not in the direction of the ranch. The driver was taking them deeper into the city.

She turned back to him. "Where are you taking me?"

"I want to show you where I live."

Julien thought the evening was going pretty well. Against his better judgment, primal instinct ruled and he feared he was about to throw caution to the wind, as it were. Ever since Renee, he'd decided to heed his most painful lessons, give credence to that adage "fool me once..." He'd promised himself to never take a risk on a woman if he had the slightest bad feeling as to the outcome.

He had that with Skylar. His gut told him being involved with her would surely result in heartbreak. Yet he could not turn away from Skylar. She was nectar to a hummingbird. Pollen to a bumblebee.

Add to that her predicament and his innate nature to protect her, and he was lost. He wouldn't turn away from her until the man who'd shot at her was found.

The sedan stopped and Julien got out before the driver, holding his hand for Skylar as he opened her door. She took it and rose up out of the back seat. He looked around as he always did—a habit he had developed during his days as a cop and a Ranger. A car parked along the street half a block down caught his immediate attention. He watched it surreptitiously. The car stayed parked and although a good distance away, the driver's head seemed turned toward them.

Julien bent back into the car and told the driver, "Wait just a second." Then he straightened and faced Skylar so that he could still see the parked car.

"What's wrong?" she asked.

"Just a minute." With another covert glance, he saw the stranger drive away. Still not convinced they were out of danger, Julien waited until the car disappeared before telling the driver to go.

Unable to shake off the uneasy feeling creeping up his neck, Julien kept Skylar in front of him to block her from whoever was in the car. What if the stranger came back?

Opening the apartment building door, he ushered her inside, trying not to let his caution alert her. Then he let go of her hand and turned to peer out the window of the closed door. He could see the car. A man got out and started walking purposefully toward the building.

"What's wrong?" Skylar asked, sounding nervous. Evidently she'd picked up on his tension.

"I'm not sure." He watched the man walk toward them, look up the tall apartment building and then at the door—as though wondering what floor they were heading to?

As the man neared, Julien left the entryway and stepped out onto the sidewalk. The man met his direct gaze. Julien wasn't sure he was the same man who had attacked Skylar. Maybe the same build, with dark hair and brown eyes.

Julien moved the lapel of his jacket to reveal his holstered pistol as he broadened his stance and squared his shoulders.

The man looked down then back up at his face, veering away. "Dude." He hurried past.

He was just a pedestrian passing by. He wasn't the attacker. The man glanced back a few times before Julien turned to reenter his apartment building.

"Who was that?" Skylar asked, anxiety clear on her face. "Is everything okay?"

"Nobody. We're safe." He put his hand on her lower back to calm her nerves and walked with her toward the elevators.

Her eyes lost their worried look and he wondered if his reassurance had done that or if it was due to his hand on her body.

After an elevator ride and short walk down the hall, he let her into his apartment on the top floor of the building.

Entering the open space of the living room, she walked immediately to the wall of windows that offered a view of downtown Dallas. Irving and Dallas were close and Julien lived in Dallas. Then she turned in a slow circle, inspecting his apartment.

"There's not much here. You live a very clutter-free life," she said.

"It's just me and, truth be told, I'm not home much. No reason to be."

She continued to study the space. "For a man who wants a family, you chose a strange place to live."

"This isn't where I would live if I had a wife and kids."

That drew her gaze to him. "Where would you live?"

"In a suburb somewhere outside the city. A neighborhood where there are other kids, maybe a community pool. I loved swimming with friends when I was growing up."

"Your farm had a pool?"

"No, but one of my friends did."

"Huh." She nodded and resumed checking out his place.

What was she thinking?

"If I was your client and asked you to redecorate my apartment, what would you do?" he asked.

"Funny you should ask." She walked toward him and stopped. "What kind of décor do you like? Old-fashioned? Modern? Themed?"

"I don't know. I've never really thought about it. Modern seems too cold. Old-fashioned too…old. Themed? I think I'd get tired of that after a while."

"Color-coordinated and cozy-modern?" she asked. "I'm sure there's a term for that." She smiled.

"If you'd gone to college for interior design, you'd know it," he said, smiling slightly so she would know he wasn't trying to be insulting.

She nodded. "Yes, I suppose I would."

"You still could, you know. Go to college."

"I'm thirty-three."

"That's young. Lots of people go to college later in life. Nobody truly knows what they want to do with their lives right out of high school."

"You did."

Skylar walked over the fireplace and he went to stand beside her, after having fallen into a lengthy admiration of her rear. "You knew what you wanted to do before you graduated high school."

She looked at him. "I thought I knew."

"You knew. You just lost your way." He didn't say *because of her father*, but her father was responsible. His bad parenting was the cause.

"I'm very happy with my life, Julien."

He didn't believe her. Well, she might be happy, but she would be happier doing what life had called her to do. He decided to test the theory.

"Design my apartment, then. You have a clean slate." He stretched his hand out to indicate the bland décor. "Don't just tell me what you'd do. Design it."

"Julien…"

"I'll pay you whatever the current rate is."

"No, you don't have to pay me. Just buy the materials. I'm not actually an interior designer."

"Okay." He faced her and stuck out his hand. "Deal."

He couldn't explain to himself why this was so important to him. He thought if Skylar did one day realize what she'd given up, she would be more open to leaving ranch life. But his motive wasn't totally selfish. He felt more than that. He honestly believed she had missed her true calling. Anyone lucky enough to know what their calling was should have the opportunity to explore it. Besides, her ranch wasn't going anywhere. It would always be there for her. She could live there and still be an interior designer. Changing professions, or even adding a new one, didn't mean she had to leave.

As he watched her study his apartment, he realized he looked forward to seeing her in action and the end result. He also looked forward to all the time they would spend together.

"This will be fun."

Skylar's bright announcement brought his focus back to her. He saw her happy face and had to reach for her hands, drawing her closer. Their kiss had a lasting effect on him. Ever since, he'd had to push back the urge to kiss her again. Seeing her smiling eyes…well, that instinct welled up again.

"You have a beautiful smile," he said.

The light in her eyes became less jovial, however, and warmed with his nearness. "You're going to have a beautiful home."

He could tell she tried to keep the moment casual. He wasn't in the mood for causal anymore. He had held himself off long enough.

Right now, he needed to find out if that kiss was a one-time thing or if their chemistry was as explosive as he imagined.

He slid his arm around her, resting his hand on her lower back.

"Julien?" Her voice sounded sultry and reactive to his initiative.

Without responding, he pulled her against him. She put both of hers hands on his chest. Then she looked there, as though the contact had kindled a heated spark. She moved her hand over his muscles and he heard her breathing quicken.

That was all he needed.

He lowered his head, seeking her mouth. She lifted her head and they kissed.

Just like the last time, instant desire ignited. She moved her hands up to wrap them around his neck and shoulders. He embraced her tighter, their bodies pressed against each other, then he deepened the kiss.

After many seconds of hungrily devouring each other, Julien felt her move her hips, as though seeking more intimacy. He didn't think. He lifted her and walked her to the couch, drawing away to lie her down.

Her eyes met his and, seeing the invitation there, he lowered himself on top of her, pressing his mouth to hers again. He felt his hardness against her and she responded with the lift of her hips. Then she broke from the kiss to breathe deeper.

He met her lustful eyes and then looked down at her breasts. He started to undress her.

"Wait." She pushed at his chest. "Wait. Oh, wait."

He understood implicitly. Desire had carried them away. He rose onto his hands, looking down at her blinking eyes and parted lips.

"What are we doing?" she asked.

She sounded alarmed.

Julien stood and she sat up on the couch, putting her face in her hands and then resting her forehead on her fingertips, chest filling and expelling.

He caught his breath, too. "I'm sorry."

Without looking at him, she stood. "I think you should take me home now."

Probably a good idea. He had set out to test their chemistry. He did not need any further testing.

The next morning, Skylar rode in silence with Julien to Wes McKann's ranch. She hadn't slept much last night. She'd worried over her reaction to Julien's kiss. It was so strong, so uncontrollable. She didn't see how she would make it through this without a broken heart. The sooner they found whoever had shot at her, the better.

The sheriff had stopped by to inform them he had spoken with the neighbors, and no one had seen anything. So far he had boot prints near the hole in the ground and tire tracks. No fingerprints and still no casings from the gunshots. It was unnerving how long this was taking. When would she be able to go anywhere without feeling like she had to look over her shoulder? Julien made her feel safe but she couldn't fool herself into banking on that one-hundred percent. She was ever grateful to have a man like him nearby, but the threat was still out there. A dangerous one.

A fiftyish woman with short dark hair and black-rimmed glasses answered Wes's door.

"Hello, is Wes home?" Julien asked.

"He's out working the ranch. Can I help you?"

Julien showed the woman his DAI identification. "I'm a private investigator looking into a missing person case. Have you seen or spoken with Mrs. McKann recently?"

The woman's eyebrows lowered. "No, I haven't. And this isn't the first time Charlotte left him."

"How do you know she left?" Julien asked.

"She wasn't here one day I came to work," the woman said.

That did not mean something terrible hadn't happened to her.

"What do you do here?" Julien asked.

"I'm their housekeeper. I sometimes cook for them, too."

"How many times has Charlotte left in the past?" Skylar asked.

The woman thought a moment. "As far as I know, just twice."

"Where did she go those times?" Julien asked.

"She has a friend, the one who reported her missing. Or she might have gone to her parents'. If she did, then she's serious about leaving him this time. Her parents live in Maine."

That was what they had been told before. The sheriff said the parents claimed Charlotte was not there.

"Why does she leave him? Are they having trouble in their marriage?" Julien asked.

The housekeeper glanced around the property, as though looking for signs of Wes. "Look, I'm not comfortable talking to you without Wes here."

"Charlotte may have been murdered," Julien said. "We're trying to find her and we need help."

"Murdered?" The housekeeper looked shocked.

"There hasn't been any activity in her banking or credit cards and she hasn't used her cell phone."

The woman put her hand to her chest. "Are you suggesting that Wes may have killed her?"

"How is their marriage, Ms...?"

"Mrs. Anderson," she said. "Cheryl Anderson."

"Mrs. Anderson," Julien said.

"Well, I'm not here at night, but I've heard them fighting in the morning sometimes. Charlotte complains about living so far from her friends and being lonely since he works such long hours. She wants to travel and have a social life. That's probably what they fight about most. Wes isn't very social. He's sort of a lone wolf."

That made sense, Skylar thought, given his surly demeanor.

"Wes isn't a bad man," Cheryl said. "He may seem as though he is, but what most people don't see is that he is a fair man. A straight shooter. I've never seen him mistreat Charlotte, either. He pays me well and is always respectful. For the life of me, I can't see him killing his wife, let alone anyone else."

"How long have you worked for him?"

"Almost ten years."

"Do you know if Charlotte ever had any affairs?" Julien asked.

Cheryl shook her head. "Like I said, I'm not here at night. I usually leave around six. If Charlotte left the house after that, I wouldn't know. I never heard her talking to anyone on the phone during the day. She would go places sometimes, but she never told me where she was going."

"Thanks, Mrs. Anderson," Julien said. "Would

it be all right if we walk around and maybe talk to a few of the other workers?"

"That's not for me to say. You should ask Wes."

"Thank you. Have a nice day."

Skylar walked with him away from the house, glancing back as they neared Julien's BMW. Cheryl had closed the door.

Julien walked past his car and headed for the stable. Apparently, he wasn't going to ask Wes's permission. Skylar doubted he would give his permission anyway. Cheryl seemed convinced Wes was incapable of harming anyone. She had acknowledged his unfriendliness, but after working for him for nearly a decade, she must know him pretty well. Maybe he hadn't killed Charlotte. Maybe there was another reason she had vanished. Like an affair gone bad.

Entering the stable, Skylar saw a young man cleaning out a stall. He stopped working as they approached.

Julien went through the introductions. The man, probably barely nineteen, was Nicholas Barnes. He had worked at the ranch for a year.

"I haven't seen Mr. McKann's wife in a while," Nicholas said. "I've heard talk that she went missing, but I didn't see anything suspicious that day."

"What about any other days?"

Nicholas leaned on his pitchfork and took a few seconds before saying, "Last summer, when I first started working here, I was getting ready to leave for the day when me and a couple of other ranch hands heard yelling coming from the big house. It was spring, so the windows were open. We could all hear them plain as day. She was hollering that his only activity was drinking alone, and he called her a spoiled bitch. They went back and forth about how she grew up rich and wanted a jet-setting lifestyle and he would never live that way. Calling each other names, until finally it got quiet. Next thing, we saw Mr. McKann getting into his truck and driving away. Folks in town said he spent a few hours at a bar and got into a fight."

That matched what they had heard about Wes so far.

"What bar was it? And do you know who he got into a fight with?" Julien asked.

"The Rusty Lantern. I don't know the man. Words were exchanged and things got ugly."

"What kind of words? Did the guy have relations with Charlotte?"

"I don't know. Apparently, the man said some things about her, though, and Wes. Something like Wes didn't deserve her. I can't remember exactly."

"Can you describe the man?" Skylar asked.

"Nah." He shook his head. "It was so fleeting."

"Anything else?" Julien asked.

"Yeah. Just about two months ago, I was out in the corral when the missus came storming out of the house. Mr. McKann was right behind her. I couldn't hear what she was ranting about, but she was all mad. Mr. McKann grabbed her arm and stopped her. She tried to get away, but he kept a hold on her. I heard her yell, 'Let go of me.' He did and she got into her car and raced off. I didn't see her for a few days after that. But then they seemed to have patched things up because about a week later, I saw him kiss her before she went somewhere. So, I guess things weren't always rocky with them. Some couples are like that. They fight as passionately as they love. I have an aunt and uncle like that."

"How is Wes to you? How does he treat everyone who works for him?" Skylar asked.

"Great. He pays us all a good wage and is always nice. Doesn't smile much. Has one of those faces you can't read, you know? If anybody messes up, though, he doesn't go easy on you. He wants things done right and has no tolerance for anyone who's lackadaisical, you know?"

Julien nodded.

"You think he hurt his wife?" Nicholas asked.

"We don't know what happened to Charlotte, but we'll find her. Thanks, Nicholas. You've been a big help."

Skylar walked with Julien to the BMW. "Everyone seems to think highly of him."

"Yes, but they also think he has an attitude."

"And he's a loner and Charlotte is a socialite. Opposites attract, but in this case, maybe it's toxic."

"Maybe."

Trotting hooves grew louder behind them. Near the BMW, Skylar stopped and turned with Julien. It was Wes and the scowl on his face said clearly that he was furious.

"What are you doing here?" Wes demanded, his horse sidestepping a few times before stilling.

"We were just asking a few questions," Julien said calmly.

"About what? About how I murdered my wife?" he snapped.

"No, about the state of your marriage. Seems things haven't been rosy between the two of you. More like *War of the Roses.*"

With his lips pursing white, Wes got off his horse and walked up to Julien, who didn't budge. They stared each other down, Julien's gaze steady and unflinching. Wes's a black thundercloud.

"My marriage is none of your damn business," Wes ground out. "I want you to stay off my property. If I see you here again, I'll call the sheriff."

Julien lifted his hands. "We have what we came for."

Wes moved forward and Skylar thought he would start swinging his fists. She stepped between the two men, putting her hand on Wes's chest. "We're going now."

He looked down and she had never seen such raw intensity in a man's eyes. She saw anger born of pain. She saw a man who struggled with too many things that didn't go the way he wished. She also saw a man who had reached his limit of endurance. And that is why she was convinced he could have killed Charlotte.

And that had been the body she had seen wrapped in plastic, just as Julien must be thinking, or he wouldn't be investigating her disappearance. The same applied to the lawyer's wife. Which body had the killer nearly buried? And where was it now?

Julien took a step back and took her hand in his.

"Hey," he said. "Don't worry. I will catch that gunman."

Skylar moved her head into his hand, appreciating that he not only saw her trepidation but put her at ease—at least as much as she could be until the killer was found.

Chapter 8

The Rusty Lantern was an upscale bar in Waldon, Texas, not far from Skylar's family ranch. Julien found it strange that Wes had chosen the place for a bender after fighting with his wife. It seemed more Charlotte's type than Wes's. Julien pictured him in something less classy, less pompous. Not a dive, but more casual.

Julien took great pleasure in walking into the Rusty Lantern with Skylar on his arm. And she was. She had her arm tucked in with his on this chilly evening. She wore jeans and a flowy white top that flirted with her waist.

He looked around as he always did and saw nothing or no one suspicious. When a young hostess approached, he spoke up immediately. "We'd like to talk with the owner or the general manager."

"Oh." Her face took on a concerned frown. "Is there a problem?"

He explained who he was and introduced Skylar. "We're here about Charlotte McKann's disappearance."

He waited and watched the hostess's reaction. She seemed not to recognize the name.

"Who?"

"Can we speak with the owner or the general manager?" Julien asked again.

"Oh, sure. Just a sec." She walked off and a few moments later a man appeared.

"Jack Burman, General Manager," he said, holding out his hand.

"Julien LaCroix, Private Investigator." He shook Jack's hand. "This is Skylar Chelsey, my...partner." Much easier to introduce her that way than to explain that she was now his constant companion because she'd been shot at.

"You're here to talk about Charlotte McKann?" Jack asked.

"Yes. In particular, we'd like to talk to the man Wes McKann got into a fight with last fall."

"Ah. We don't see that in this bar very often. We attract a more sophisticated crowd. From what

I heard, Wes normally goes to Schmidt's on the other side of town," Jack said.

Schmidt's wasn't an establishment in ill repair, but there was no comparison to the Rusty Lantern. It suited Wes's personality.

"Did he have a reason for being here that night?" Julien needed to confirm what Nicholas had told them.

"Benson Davett comes in on occasion. That night he was here with a colleague when Wes showed up. Wes sat at the bar awhile, drinking whiskey. He wasn't drinking heavily, but he kept looking over at Ben's table. He settled his tab and I thought he was going to leave, but he stopped at Ben's table. I didn't hear what was said, but one of the waitresses heard them. Wes told Ben to stay away from his wife. Ben said he didn't know what Wes was talking about. Wes said Charlotte admitted to having an affair with him. Ben kept denying it, which angered Wes. He leaned down and grabbed Ben by the shirt, all but lifting him out of his chair, and told him to stop lying."

Julien remembered the ranch hand's remarks. Wes and Charlotte must have been arguing about that when Nicholas heard them yelling.

"Ben shoved his hand away and stood up. The two faced off," Jack said. "Wes said he followed his wife to the Daisies Inn and watched Ben go to her room. Ben said he didn't have to answer to Wes and it wasn't his fault he couldn't hang on to his woman. That's when Wes hit him—clocked him good on the jaw. Ben fought back, but Wes is a big, strong man. He had him on the ground. One of my kitchen managers helped me pull him off."

"Did Ben press charges?" Julien asked.

"No. I told Wes to leave and don't come back. We can't have that kind of behavior in this bar."

Julien nodded. Well, Wes had ample motive to kill his wife. Except, why wait all those months? Had it taken him that long to plan the deed?

"Ben Davett's wife is missing, too," Julien said.

Both Charlotte and Audrey had vanished. Julien did not think that was a coincidence, not after hearing this story.

The next day, Skylar arrived back home after a long day of work. Julien had arranged for a bodyguard to accompany her while he delved into Audrey Davett's case.

The bodyguard had gone home and Skylar entered her house, finding Julien in the kitchen with two open laptops. His shirt was unbuttoned at the top and partially untucked from his jeans. He looked like he had worked hard, too. Seeing her, he shut down the computers.

"How was your day?" he asked as he stood.

He caught her unprepared when he came to her and kissed her. Then he took a step back as though he had surprised himself. That quick zing of desire nearly had her forgetting how hungry she was.

"Good. Yours?" She went to the refrigerator.

"I spoke with the detective assigned to Audrey Davett's case. A video camera at the mall showed her arriving and leaving the day she disappeared."

Skylar took out some leftover Chinese and held up the two containers in silent question.

"Sure," he said.

She put them in the microwave.

"Detective Sidney said Benson called the police when he got home late from work and Audrey wasn't there," Julien said.

Skylar took two waters out of the fridge and handed one to him. "No one else has seen her after that?"

"No. And Benson was at work during that time. Sidney confirmed that."

"Did he have a nice life insurance policy on her?"

"I don't know that yet. Sidney didn't check since Benson was at work and had a solid alibi."

Skylar thought the detective should have checked anyway. "Benson might have paid somebody. Did Audrey know he was having an affair with Wes's wife?"

"I don't know. Sidney is getting access to Audrey's financial records. He's also going to look into Charlotte's. He'll call when he has them."

"How could the two disappearances be related?" she asked.

"I've been going over this in my head all day. Benson had an affair with Charlotte. Maybe he killed her after she threatened him in some way. Scar his reputation...expose his infidelity to his wife."

"But why harm Audrey if he meant to keep her from finding out about his affair?" she asked.

"Maybe she did find out. Jack Burman said Benson denied any affair with Charlotte and got defensive when Wes pressed him."

Skylar might believe Benson would be compelled to kill his wife to protect his reputation, but Audrey had been alive when Wes confronted him. The secret was out. There had to be another reason Benson would murder her—if, in fact, he had. She'd put her money on a sizable life insurance policy. And if the lawyer offed Wes's wife, he did it because Charlotte had found out about his plan.

"I still think, if anybody killed Charlotte, it was Wes," she said.

"Right now, I'd have to agree, but I need to know how—or if—her disappearance is related to Audrey's.

"Speaking of which." He held up a sticky note with a number written on it. "I'm going to call her parents."

Skylar removed the food from the microwave

and put the carton in front of him with a fork. "After dinner." She went to the table, sitting opposite his closed laptops.

He sat adjacent to her. "Dinner with my lady." He grinned at her and then took a bite.

His lady? He had sure taken to treating her like his girlfriend. "It's nice not eating alone." As a single person, she often ate standing up at the kitchen counter.

"It's nice eating with you," he said.

"Be careful what you say. This might turn into something neither one of us can walk away from."

"Maybe we won't want to walk away."

And who would do the moving if that happened?

Julien took a cup of steaming tea from Skylar and put it on the coffee table. She sat beside him, sipping and looking at the news program on television. He took out his cell, keyed in Charlotte's parents' home number and put his phone to his ear. Lisa and Gerald Campbell lived in Bangor, Maine.

Lisa answered. Julien explained who he was and asked if Charlotte was there.

"No, she isn't. A detective called a few days ago and we told him the same thing. Wes called, also."

"When is the last time you saw or spoke with her?" Julien asked.

"Oh, probably a little more than a week ago. She

and Wes were having trouble. It's not unlike her to get away and take some time to think."

"She's done that before?"

"Yes. Not in a while, but she has."

Lisa did not sound worried about her daughter. Could it be that Charlotte's friend had overreacted when she'd called in the missing person report? Julien's gut told him no.

"And she does this to get away from Wes?" he asked.

"He can be challenging to live with. Wes is not the friendliest man alive. He has no sense of humor and he never shows affection."

What about Charlotte? Julien wondered how much she contributed to the failing marriage.

"Why hasn't she divorced him?" he asked.

"Well, I suspect that is only a matter of time. She did love him when they first got together and she's never stopped being attracted to him. But they just haven't been able to get along outside the bedroom. I've told her sex isn't enough to make a happy marriage. I've encouraged her to end it."

So, if Charlotte had gone somewhere to give herself some space, her dilemma was whether she could give up great sex or not.

Julien glanced at Skylar. He was pretty sure the two of them could have both.

"What does Wes want?" he asked Lisa.

"He claims to love her and doesn't want a divorce. He's talked her out of it every time she's brought up the subject."

That didn't sound like a man who wanted his wife dead. Unless the last fight they'd had was when Charlotte told him she was filing for a divorce. Wes might be one of those men who refused to allow any other man to have his woman if he couldn't.

"You said Wes contacted you?"

"Yes. He's called three or four times looking for Charlotte."

Was Wes convinced she had gone to her parents' house? How far would the Campbells go to prevent him from contacting her? And if they were trying to prevent contact, why?

"Is Charlotte afraid of Wes?" he asked.

With the lengthy silence on the other end of the call, Julien knew Lisa contemplated her reply.

"At times, yes. They fought all the time."

Julien didn't miss how she'd said "fought" and not "fight," as though she already knew Wes and Charlotte were a thing of the past.

"Why was she afraid of him? Did he hurt her?"

"No. He never hit her, but when they got into arguments, he yelled. That temper is what scared her."

Julien needed to find out if Lisa was protecting her daughter by lying about her whereabouts.

"Based on what you've told me, I think there's

enough to open a possible homicide investigation, with Wes being the prime suspect," he said.

"Oh. Murder..." She exhaled as though anxious. "You think Charlotte was *murdered*?"

"Mrs. Campbell, we're looking for a missing person, but there're reasons she is missing and one of those could be murder. I don't mean to be disrespectful, but I'm wondering if you're telling me everything—in particular, what you know about where your daughter is right now."

"I—I don't know."

"Wes McKann will be investigated. There's a detective assigned to Charlotte's case. That costs more than money, Mrs. Campbell. It consumes time that could be spent on other investigations. So, if you know something, I suggest you tell me."

"I'll be sure and do that," Lisa said.

Julien ended the call and met Skylar's inquisitive gaze.

"You think Charlotte is there, don't you?" Skylar said.

"I think it's a distinct possibility." He stretched his arm across the back of the sofa.

"It's also possible that he killed her."

"Maybe. It's my job to look at every possibility."

She angled her head toward him as she met his eyes. "And you wouldn't work for an agency like DAI if you weren't good at your job."

He appreciated the compliment but didn't acknowledge it. He did what he did for the defenseless. He knew Skylar was convinced Wes killed his wife, but Julien didn't think he'd be stupid enough to try to bury her so close to River Rock Ranch's property line. Whoever had done that must not have known the area very well, much less that Skylar or one of her workers checked the fence on a regular basis. It must have been someone who knew little or nothing about ranching, and certainly not someone who owned the property. Someone who had come upon a remote area and thought it would make a good gravesite.

Skylar leaned her head back against his arm. The contact, however innocent, made him aware of her, the slope of her nose, her long lashes and full lips. Even in her flannel shirt, he could make out the tempting shape of her breasts.

She moved her head just then, catching him, and he found himself in the perfect position to kiss her. More and more he felt himself giving in to the desire to see where this attraction would lead. He could throw caution out the window and let himself get involved with her. If it turned serious, they would have to find a way to work things out. And if they couldn't, then they would have to say goodbye. While he didn't like that possibility, he also couldn't resist the moment.

He put his lips to hers and that same steamy passion came over him. With the catch of her breath, he knew she had the same reaction.

Julien decided not to hold back. He kissed her deeper.

She slid her hand up his chest, inflaming him even more. He moved forward, urging her back onto the sofa. She lifted her legs onto the cushions and he came down on top of her, tasting her as he kissed her with all the desire he felt, holding himself up on one elbow. She sank her fingers into his hair. He ran his hand down to her breasts, having longed to do so for a while now.

He kissed her neck. She smelled like outdoors and horses. He never thought he would find that alluring, but with Skylar, it was. She intoxicated him.

She found her way inside his shirt and her hands ran over his chest.

He began to unbutton her shirt. He parted the sides and unclasped her bra. She had unbuttoned his shirt and now pushed it off his shoulders.

With her hands going to his back, he held her breast and put his mouth around her nipple. She tipped her head back, eyes closed, and breathed faster.

He kissed her other breast and then rose onto his knees, straddling her. He began to unbutton his jeans. She watched him with a dazed look. Then reason began to flow into her eyes.

She was going to stop him. He knew it. Just when every molecule in him wanted her.

"Skylar, we—"

"—have to stop." She bent her knees, scooted back and then got to her feet. "This is crazy."

That was one word to describe it.

He refastened his jeans, literally aching for her. He stood and went to her as she finished buttoning her shirt.

"Skylar, I've never been with a woman who turns me on as much as you do. I don't even know why."

"I don't know…" She rubbed her arms and walked over to the window. "I'm afraid once we take it to the next level, it will only end badly."

"Have you ever been with a man who makes you feel like you just did on that sofa?" he asked, walking up behind her.

Several seconds passed. "No. And that's what scares me."

"It scares me, too, but I'm willing to take a chance." He could fall in love with her and face losing her, but that didn't matter right now.

She turned to him. "I don't know if I am. If we start to have strong feelings for each other, we'll be forced to make huge life-changing decisions, and I'm not prepared for that."

He wasn't, either, but…

"Not many people have the kind of chemistry we do," he said. "You're willing to pass that up?"

She met his eyes and he could see her inner turmoil. "Right now, yes."

Maybe she had a valid point. Maybe she would save him a lot of misery by cooling things off. But what if he was already doomed? If he did fall in love with her, would he be in a lot of pain if he had to leave her? More pain than he had ever felt before? What if neither one of them could control this? Next time they might not be able to stop. What then?

Chapter 9

Skylar jolted awake to the sound of the security alarm going off. Last night, Julien did his usual final check of the day for suspicious activity outside her house and there was none. He had installed motion detectors, as well, and that was what had set off the alarm. She tossed the covers aside and grabbed her robe. Leaving her room, she saw a shirtless Julien racing down the stairs with his gun drawn.

She cautiously followed.

He checked the alarm next to the front door, glancing back as she approached.

"Something's outside," he said, silencing the alarm. "The garage motion detector was triggered."

She went to the big front window and peeked out, seeing the motion detector had turned on a bright light.

"Stay here. I'm going to go check outside."

She waited near the front window, not seeing any movement other than him walking stealthily toward the garage. He checked inside and reappeared, going around her truck, looking in the cab and underneath. He stopped at the bed of her truck, then hurried back into the house.

"Call 9-1-1."

"What did you find?" she asked, following him to the kitchen where there was a landline.

"There's a backpack in the bed of your truck that wasn't there last night."

A backpack. What on earth? She called 9-1-1, watching Julien navigate on his phone, probably reviewing the video recording that triggered the alarm.

She spoke with the dispatcher, who informed her someone would be there shortly. She disconnected as Julien went back up to his bedroom. A moment later, he reappeared, having added a shirt to his jeans. He carried something other than his gun. She couldn't tell what it was. Some sort of handheld rectangular device.

He went back outside, scanning the area first, his gun ready. Back at the truck, he wiped something on the backpack and then inserted it into the device.

Then he returned to the house, a grave, flat line to his mouth and concern setting his brow low over his eyes.

"There's an explosive in that bag," he said, closing the door.

Someone had intended for her to get in her truck and the device would have exploded? Was the person watching her movements? Would they then detonate the bomb?

"I don't think they planned on being interrupted by the alarm," Julien said. He headed for the door again. "Stay here and lock this door until the police get here. I'm going to search the property again."

He left and the sound of a siren grew louder. While Julien vanished, the sheriff's vehicle appeared.

Skylar waited for him to reach the porch and then unlocked and opened the door. "There's a bomb in a backpack in the bed of my truck."

"Is everyone all right?"

"Yes. Julien went to search the property. He'll be back in a few minutes." She hoped. She worried he'd encounter the intruder and get himself hurt. Or killed. Just the mere possibility gave her a heavy feeling in her stomach.

Sheriff McKenzie used his phone to call in some bomb experts.

"We can talk inside," she said, leading him into

her house. She went about making a pot of coffee while he finished talking to his team.

"Tell me what happened," the sheriff said.

"We were awakened by the sound of the security alarm. Julien went outside and found a backpack. He did a test that confirmed it was some sort of bomb."

"Has anything else happened since the night the intruder tried to attack you?" he asked.

She shook her head, then remembered. "I fired my deputy ranch manager, but I doubt he would plant a bomb in my truck." She poured two cups of coffee, then brought them to the kitchen island along with some creamer.

"Tell me about him. What's his name?" He took out a notepad and pen from his jacket.

"Shawn Bellarmine. I fired him for mistreating my livestock. When I took over the ranch operations, he had to step down as manager and take the deputy position. He never really adjusted after that. I could always sense some animosity."

"People seek revenge for lesser offenses," the sheriff said. "I'll follow up and ask him some questions."

She remembered what Marko had told her and Julien about Shawn's girlfriend. "One of my workers said Shawn had a girlfriend no one has seen in a while," she said. "Her name is Felicia Montague. Julien is looking for her."

He wrote the name down and then looked back at the security system panel. "Can I have a look at the recording?"

"Go ahead."

She followed him. As they reached the door, it opened and Julien appeared. "He got away," he said.

The sheriff played back the recording. She saw someone approach the truck in a hoodie and a mask. When the motion detector triggered the light and the alarm, the man dumped the bag and ran off, disappearing into darkness.

"The mask looks the same as the one the intruder wore," she said. "He seems about the same height and build, too."

"What about the man who shot at you?" the sheriff asked.

"Could be the same. That man was farther away, though. I can't say for sure. I didn't get a good look at him." She had been too busy racing to get away from him.

"After the intruder attacked you, I had a team do a much more thorough search for shell casings. They did eventually find two," the sheriff said.

Skylar was grateful that he had given the incident his full attention.

"I've opened an investigation to find out if whoever the man was had intended to bury a body and covered his tracks by burying a bag of trash instead," the sheriff said. "My only hesitation is that he wouldn't have had time to go get a bag of trash and bury it before I showed up with my deputies."

"He may have had it with him as contingency," Julien said.

"That's possible."

"Are you sure there was no body under the bag of trash?" Skylar asked.

"Yes. I saw for myself," the sheriff said. "Only bare ground."

The man had decided not to bury the body there, which meant he had disposed of it elsewhere. But where? she asked herself.

The sheriff turned to Julien. "I suggest we start working together on this. You share anything you find and I'll share what I find. If we have a killer out there, I want him found."

Julien nodded his head once. "I agree."

Sheriff McKenzie went out to meet the bomb experts. Julien didn't follow. Instead, he faced Skylar, putting his hands on her shoulders.

"I think we should go stay at my place until this is over."

Leave the ranch? She couldn't do that. There'd be no ranch manager.

"I've been thinking about this a lot," Julien said. "And I found a qualified ranch manager. My resources at DAI found him."

"What?" He had done all of that without telling her?

"I didn't tell you until now because I wasn't sure we would need to go to that extreme. But I do now. A bomb was in your truck."

"Julien, I…" She put her hand to her head.

"It will only be temporary. You can spend a few days with the manager and then we'll go. This attacker won't know where you are. He won't know where I live. And the security there is good."

He had valid points. She was vulnerable here, even with security. Just working the ranch was dangerous, since she was out in the open most of the day. The killer could be lurking anywhere.

"All right. Bring in your manager." She wasn't sure what she had just signed up for, but she could not argue with his logic.

Without work to occupy her days, she and Julien would be spending a lot of one-on-one time together. Given their explosive chemistry, that might prove just as dangerous to her peace of mind.

A few days later, Julien let Skylar get settled in his guest room. He suspected she needed some space, time to adjust to her new living arrangement. While he had said it was temporary, he couldn't deny the fantasy of it not being that. She had finished orienting the manager on her ranch and now they were focused on determining if there was any connection between the missing person investigations and the man who kept trying to kill her.

She appeared from her room and joined him in the living room, sitting on the opposite end of the sofa.

"I know a good deli. We could pick something up for lunch," he told her. "Okay?"

"Sure."

She sounded stiff and uncomfortable. But before he could say anything else, his cell rang. Seeing it was the sheriff, he answered, putting it on Speaker.

"I went to talk to Wes this morning. Just got back to the office," Sheriff McKenzie said. "He claims he was working the ranch the morning Skylar saw a man digging. He also said he is fairly certain his wife has left him and is staying in hiding because she didn't want him to try to follow her."

"Do you believe him?" Julien asked.

"He could just be saying that," Skylar said.

"Oh, hello, Skylar. I didn't know you were on the call."

"Sorry," Julien answered. "I put you on speaker and figured she would want to hear what you had to say."

"That's fine. Wes admitted he and his wife have been having problems. She wanted to move closer to her parents, but Wes couldn't accommodate her because of his ranch."

That was close to what they had been told already. Wes and Charlotte's marriage was on a collision course with divorce.

"I also questioned some of Wes's workers and none could say they saw Wes or knew where he was during that time frame," the sheriff said.

"He let you?" Skylar asked.

"He didn't seem to like the idea but he didn't try to stop me. I didn't get a sense that he was trying to hide anything. He seemed more reluctant to have his personal affairs aired. He's not a very public man."

Though Julien agreed, he could see Skylar resist any notion that Wes hadn't done something terrible to his wife. Julien didn't have a definitive opinion either way. Not yet. Sheriff McKenzie was well on board with them on this case. It was good to know they had him as a resource. Julien could skirt the rules only so far, although he was willing if it meant saving a life.

A fleeting thought of Sawyer came to mind. How was he doing? The boy had not called.

After the call ended, he looked over at Skylar.

"I still think he killed her," she said.

Damn if he didn't love her bluntness. Her spirited nature. "I know you do. We will find out what happened to her."

Her mouth curved and her eyes warmed. He needed no words for her to convey her gratitude.

He patted the couch cushion. "Come here. You're too far away."

She eyed him a moment but then scooted closer. "Why do you want me closer?"

He put his arm around her and slid her right up against him. "I just do. I can't explain it."

"I can't explain why I like it, either." She rested her head on his shoulder. "I suppose, since I'm going to be staying here, I could start on decorating your house."

"Yes. You could."

"That will keep me occupied and distracted from you." Lifting her head, she smiled up at him.

"Yes, but I won't be distracted." He'd be there watching her. Wanting her.

As they met each other's eyes, Skylar's smile faded. That magical heat flared and he instantly needed to kiss her. Her gaze fell to his mouth, too.

He leaned in and touched her lips with his, light and feathery at first then, loving the taste of them, he angled his mouth over hers, going deeper and wondering if this would be the time they made it to the bedroom. More and more, he yearned to know if they'd be as good in there as they were at kissing.

Skylar began unbuttoning his shirt and he reached for her top, lifting it up and over her head. Then she moved to straddle him, looping her arms around his shoulders. He felt her breasts against him.

He slid his fingers into her hair at the back of her head and drew her to him, kissing her with all the passion burning in him. She met him with equal fervor. When Julien could take no more without going to the next level, Skylar pulled back.

He looked into her feverish eyes and watched her struggle to regain control. Oh, no. She was going to stop this again.

"What if we just did this to see what happens?" she asked breathlessly.

Had he heard her correctly? She contemplated having sex with him. "I don't think we can avoid it." And he truly believed that. Their attraction was too strong.

"But if we do…there will be no erasing it."

If the sex was as good as he suspected it would be, they would either be headed for a very serious relationship or would deal with a difficult decision. Would they walk away? "No. But if we don't, we will never know if what we have going is as good as it seems."

"We might not be able to stop," she said, sounding apprehensive.

"Is that a bad thing?" he asked.

She took her lower lip between her teeth as she decided, making him yearn to carry her off to his bed.

"I vote for seeing where this goes," he said, bringing her head back to his and kissing her.

He knew her vote when she cupped his face and

lowered her head to kiss him, holding him while their tongues danced.

As fate would have it, his cell rang at that moment.

Breaking away from the kiss, he looked at Skylar, feeling her asking the same question he posed to himself. Should he answer?

He leaned to see his phone on the coffee table. It was the social worker.

"It's Tracy Compton," he said.

Skylar climbed off him, reaching for her shirt as he answered.

"Mr. LaCroix, I'm going to visit Sawyer and he said he would like you to be there, as well. It's all cleared with his parents. Maybe you can get him to open up about his living situation."

Or maybe Sawyer was ready to talk. "I'll have to bring Skylar. Is that all right?"

"Yes, as long as she doesn't interfere."

"Great." They arranged to meet at the deli where Julien had already planned to take Skylar.

When he disconnected, he saw Skylar had put her top back on. It was just as well. They had an appointment in an hour. He preferred to have all the time he needed to savor every inch of her.

At Nettie's Café, Skylar slid in beside Julien on the booth seat, across from Tracy and Sawyer. She didn't see any marks on the boy, though he was wearing a long-sleeved shirt with a high neckline.

"It's good to see you again," Julien said to him.

"It's good to see you, too," Sawyer responded.

"How are things at home?" Tracy asked.

"Good." Sawyer lowered his gaze to his glass of soda. "My parents are being nice to me."

Because they had to, Skyler thought. But how long would that last? For as long as Child Protective Services was involved, no doubt.

"But they've not been nice in the past, right?" Julien asked.

Sawyer looked at him. "They were okay."

"It's normal for parents to discipline you when you do things that are wrong, Sawyer," Tracy said, "but not to physically or mentally hurt you."

Again the boy averted his gaze.

"I won't let your parents hurt you, Sawyer," Julien said.

"You can come stay with us until Tracy finds you a good family. If it is okay with the case worker, of course," Skylar said, surprising herself. She felt sure she wanted that for this boy—and for Julien. She knew how much he cared about him and Skylar would help if she could.

"Thanks. I liked it at your house," Sawyer said then looked at Julien. "That's why I wanted to talk to you. I wanted to thank you for getting me from my uncle's house. I didn't see it then, but I do now. He isn't a kid person."

Skylar hadn't felt like a kid person before she'd met Julien, but for some weird reason, he was changing that.

"You're welcome," Julien said. "The door is always open for you."

Sawyer smiled and looked from him to Skylar. "If I didn't have my parents, I'd want you to be mine."

Julien smiled. "Skylar and I aren't together that way."

"Yes, you are."

"No. I'm a private investigator, working on a case that involves her," Julien said.

Skylar couldn't tell if he was so insistent to ease her mind or Sawyer's.

"You act like you're married," Sawyer said.

Did they? Skylar glanced at Julien, who met her eyes.

"The way you talk to each other and look at each other reminds me of my best friend's parents. They're always talking nice to each other and kissing and touching."

Skylar had to take a moment to absorb that insight. Was that how she was reacting to Julien? She recognized how he heated her blood with just a kiss or a look, but she couldn't recall an instance of that happening in front of Sawyer. It had to be something different. Maybe their tone of voice or body language? She supposed she wasn't conscious of the way she looked at him all the time.

"Your parents don't have that?" Tracy asked.

Sawyer slowly turned to her, clearly realizing what he had opened up. "No."

At least he was honest.

"You said they fight," Tracy said. "How often is that?"

"Not often." Sawyer abruptly stood. "I just wanted to thank them. I have, and now I want to go home."

He was so defensive with questions about his parents. Skylar had a knot in her stomach. She was sure Sawyer's parents had mistreated him and saw no reason why they would suddenly change their behavior.

"Do you still have my card?" Julien asked.

"Yeah," Sawyer said grumpily, then turned and walked toward the exit.

Tracy didn't force him to come back. She stood, as well, looking from Skylar to Julien. "I'm sorry for dragging you all the way here. This isn't how I planned it to go." She grabbed her purse. "Well, unfortunately, I'm going to be forced to close this case. Without any evidence, we can't remove him from the home."

Skylar was afraid of that. Something terrible

would have to happen and Sawyer would be the one to suffer the most.

After Tracy went after Sawyer, she spent a few seconds lingering on those thoughts. Then she picked up the menu. "Well, we're here. We might as well grab something to eat."

Julien picked up his menu. "You might consider that Sawyer may feel it would be worse for him to be removed from the house than to stay," she said, playing devil's advocate. In truth, every part of her suspected Sawyer was living a child's nightmare.

"Yeah," Julien said after a while, sounding reluctant.

The waitress arrived and took their orders. Skylar drank some water and caught Julien looking at her. His expression had changed from the somber one his worry had conjured to something much warmer.

Skylar felt herself shying away from that. She recalled their kisses earlier. She had lost control. Now she needed to set some boundaries.

"About before..." she began.

"Tracy's timing was awful," he said with a grin that promised more of what Tracy had interrupted.

"Julien, it would be a mistake if we had sex." She had to blurt it out. He had to know they were setting themselves up for disaster if they gave in to their mind-numbing temptation.

"You didn't think that when you got on top of

me," he said in a low voice, leaning forward as he talked.

She sent him a wry look, unable to resist his frankness. She liked it.

"You have to know that whatever we have is overpowering," she said, her flirtation coming out in her tone automatically. This was exactly why she had climbed on top of him.

His grin renewed. "Yes."

"And that it's just sexual," she said.

"Maybe."

How could he say maybe? They didn't know each other well.

With her continued silence, he said, "I like you and we get along just fine when we aren't kissing. It's not just when our defenses fail and this red-hot chemistry takes over."

He thought they got along well? She supposed they did. No, she *knew* they did. She just didn't want to acknowledge that. A scared feeling nipped at her.

"I've spent my entire life on River Rock Ranch," she said. "Ranching is what I know. City living is alien to me." Why did she sound as though she were trying to persuade herself instead of Julien? When he didn't respond, clearly just letting her think out loud, she went on. "Your apartment doesn't feel like home to me."

"Then make it feel like home."

What was he saying? Why would he want her to make his apartment feel like her home? Because he planned to see where this led? Because he intended to get her into bed?

"I won't be put in a position where I have to choose between my ranch and you, Julien. We would both have to be crazy to let this run its course."

"Crazy? Or brave?" he asked.

"All right. Say we do have an affair. What if we fall in love?"

She saw him nearly flinch at that. His eyes blinked and he moved back a fraction, as though he hadn't thought of that possibility yet.

"What if we can't stand the idea of living apart?" she asked, pressing him further.

He had no answer. He just looked at her, dumbfounded, and her heart sank.

How many people had this much bad luck? Someone was trying to kill her and it appeared she had found the perfect man she couldn't have.

Chapter 10

Shawn refused to talk to Julien, but his girlfriend, Felicia, worked at Maxine's in Waldon. Julien took Skylar with him, of course. She had spent the morning picking out items for his apartment. She had also been on the phone numerous times with the temporary ranch manager. He was doing fine, but she was micromanaging. He hoped she would learn to let go. If she did, maybe she'd be more open to living somewhere other than her family ranch. He couldn't help thinking that she needed to experience life away from it before she could truly decide if that was where she wanted to spend the rest of her life.

He also had to deliberately caution himself not to get too sold on that idea. Ranching was in her blood. She loved what she did at River Rock Ranch. The remarkable chemistry they had made it worth his time and effort to convince her there were other options. She didn't have to completely give up the ranch, for one thing. It belonged to her family. It wasn't going anywhere.

As for having a family, he didn't trust her to come around in that regard. And it was so important to him. He really did want a family. After the crushing disappointment with Renee, he feared being wrong again. But if he didn't push Skylar, he was afraid she'd go back to her everyday routine at the ranch and try to forget him. Would she be able to? Even after the short period of time they had been together, Julien would never forget her. And if things fell apart because Skylar refused to compromise, he would always wonder *what-if.*

He held the door of Maxine's for her, then approached the young man standing at the cash register, finishing up checking out a patron. There were only two tables occupied.

"Have a seat anywhere," the young man said.

Julien explained who he was and asked if Felicia Montague still worked there.

"No, she quit a couple of weeks ago."

That was around the time Skylar had seen the man digging. "Did she say where she was going?"

"She said she was moving back in with her mother. Apparently they were estranged for several years and patched things up."

"Where does her mother live?"

"I didn't ask. She sort of left me in a lurch. No notice. Just quit." The young man must be the general manager.

"Did you know her boyfriend, Shawn Bellarmine?" Julien asked.

"No. I didn't know she had a boyfriend. I don't ask about my employee's personal lives."

"Why are you asking about Felicia?" a woman asked from behind them.

Julien turned with Skylar to see a woman approach, carrying a pot of coffee, having just filled the patrons' cups.

"We're following up on a missing person case." Julien didn't think it was necessary to go into much detail.

"Felicia is missing?"

"That's what we need to find out. How well do you know her?"

"Not well. I mean, we talked at work, but we never hung out together," the blonde woman said.

"Did she ever mention her boyfriend?" Skylar asked.

"Shawn? Yeah. She talked about him a lot. He was a jerk. In fact, that's the main reason she left town."

"Why was he the main reason?" Julien asked.

"He was a control freak. He would get mad every time she did things with her friends. He made her take this job because she wouldn't have to work nights. He was a piece of work."

"Did he ever harm her in any way?"

"No. He was just temperamental. She liked him when he wasn't going berserk, but it got to the point where she couldn't take it anymore. Besides, her mom contacted her and wanted her to move back home. They drifted apart when Felicia graduated from high school. Her mom didn't like the guy she was with—the one before Shawn. I guess Felicia realized her mom was right. She didn't exactly choose the good ones, you know?"

"Where does her mother live? And do you know her name?"

"Santa Fe, New Mexico. I don't know her mom's name, sorry."

Julien thanked both the manager and the waitress and he and Skylar left.

He had a feeling something was on her mind and was proved right when she stepped outside and said, "I don't think Shawn would plant a bomb in my truck. And the attacks on me and the bomb have to be the work of the same person."

"Felicia left around the same time you saw the digger," Julien pointed out.

"That has to be a coincidence. Besides, Felicia moved in with her mother. She isn't missing."

Julien didn't have a strong feeling Shawn was the bomb planter, either, but he had to confirm Felicia was all right. He called DAI and asked one of their professional trackers to find Felicia's mother.

"As long as we're out and about, let's go talk to the lawyer." Julien opened the door of his BMW for her.

"Okay." She got in and he drove them there.

Benson Davett had an office in a high-rise building in Dallas. Sparsely but modernly decorated, it gave the appearance of swank, as one might expect in a lawyer's office. And since the name of the firm was Davett and McDermott, he was also a partner. A successful attorney could have a lot to lose if he killed his wife, Julien told himself.

Benson stood from behind his desk, leaning over with an offered hand. "My assistant says you two are private investigators." He had a somewhat loud voice and a commanding presence, with short dark hair and direct brown eyes.

Julien shook his hand and then Benson shook Skylar's.

"Julien is," she said. "I have a vested interest in the case."

He offered them two seats opposite his desk then sat himself. "How can I help you?"

"We're looking into a couple of missing person cases and your wife's came to my attention."

Something clouded Benson's eyes and, no longer so commanding, his voice lowered as he said, "It's been two weeks and the police still haven't found her."

He had to be losing hope she would ever be found. Julien worked with people like that all the time. If someone wasn't found within two days, the odds of finding the person alive kept diminishing.

"I'm working with the sheriff now, so maybe we'll get somewhere," he said.

"Julien is an investigator with Dark Alley Investigations, so you're in good hands," Skylar said.

Benson looked from her to Julien. "I haven't heard of that agency."

"It's the most prominent and successful P.I. firm in the country," she said.

"Oh, well, then I am lucky to have you on my side." Benson smiled slightly, not a real smile. He seemed to carry a constant worry underneath his professional veneer.

"I know you've already talked to the police," Julien said, "but it would help me if you could go over the time you last saw your wife and what she was doing when she vanished."

"Of course. I last saw Audrey that morning before I left for work. She said she was going shopping that afternoon. She liked to go to her favorite mall, Uptown Park. She left the mall at about five, but she never made it home."

That corroborated what the video surveillance had revealed. Also, his paralegal, Maria Morales, confirmed to the police—with whom Julien kept in contact and had an excellent rapport—he was at work until after seven that night. No one else could say exactly when Benson left that day.

"Mr. Davett, do you know of anyone in your wife's life who didn't like her? Was there anyone she had any kind of conflict with?"

"Not to my knowledge. She had many friends, was active in charities."

"Were the two of you close?"

Benson leaned back and put his curled fingers beneath his chin, elbow on the armrest. "We were when we first got married. I have to be honest and say, as the years went by, we grew apart. I suppose that's what happens to most couples. After the passion fades, you become best friends, companions. We have a comfortable relationship. With my work here at the firm, I'm not home much. Now that she's missing, I wish I hadn't spent so much time away from her."

He seemed sincere. "The case file said she usually had a driver take her places. Why did she drive herself that particular day?"

"Our driver took the day off. His wife had a baby."

Julien nodded. He had asked enough questions. "Thank you for your time." He stood and so did Skylar.

"I hope you have better luck than the police did," Benson said, standing, as well.

"I'll do my best."

He and Skylar left the office, stopping along the way to question a few of the workers. Most had been there for years and had nothing but glowing accolades for Benson and his partner. They were both ethical lawyers with stellar reputations. *Sleazy* was not a word used to describe them, or anything close to that.

His cell rang and he saw it was DAI. He answered, and told by the tracker working on finding Felicia that she had been with her mother and was alive and well.

"Felicia is all right."

"That is a relief. One less person to worry about," Skylar said.

"Wes McKann is looking guiltier and guiltier," Julien said after they left the building.

"I knew it."

"Now we just have to find Charlotte." Or whatever was left of her.

Why she had agreed to this, Skylar didn't know. She studied herself in the bathroom mirror. No denying it—she had dressed for Julien. The shape-hugging black dress dipped low at the neckline and flared slightly below the hip. She had chosen three-inch black heels and a delicate diamond necklace with matching earrings and bracelet. The ring on her right hand was a humble garnet. She seldom wore jewelry like this and it felt good. Feminine.

After a couple of days cooped up in the apartment, she leaned on that excuse for deciding to go out on a date with Julien. He no doubt planned on citifying her some more.

Giving her stylishly pinned-up hair a few mists of fragranced spray, she left the bathroom. Emerging into the living room, she saw Julien standing with his back to her before the fireplace. He turned when he must have heard her. When he went still and his eyes devoured her, she knew her efforts had paid off.

"Wow," he said. "You're stunning."

"You clean up nice, too." He had on a black suit with a tie that subtly changed to a deep green color as the light changed.

He continued to stand there and stare.

Growing uncomfortable, unaccustomed to this much attention, she said, "Ready?"

He cleared his throat. "Yes."

All the way to the restaurant, Julien kept glancing over at her. Skylar began to regret dressing up. The evening could only end one way if it started like this.

A hostess took them to their reserved table, a window seat with a view of the Mandalay Canals. It really was quite lovely. She forgot how her glamorous appearance affected Julien and gave herself over to the evening.

"You're dressing up like this pretty often," Julien said.

He must think she was a cowgirl all the time. "I go to parties with my family and friends." Her parents knew a lot of prominent people. They threw parties at their house and went to others. "I go to plays and charity dinners."

"What kinds of charities?"

"Alzheimer's. Homelessness. Cancer. As many as I can."

He regarded her as though she might be a martyr.

Not all the events she attended were that pure on her part. "Lately my mother has been inviting me to many events. She thinks she's my matchmaker."

He took a sip of his water. "I wouldn't have thought you were a play-going kind of woman."

"I like the costumes and the creativity of the stage," she replied. "But my favorite events are festivals. In fact, there's a food truck festival coming up, with a country and western band and a carnival."

He chuckled. "Now that's more in line with what I envisioned for you."

The way he smiled and the seductive look in his

eyes stopped her for a moment. She felt warmth infuse her entire body.

"What do you like to do in your free time?" she asked.

"I like going to community events. I like to read, and it's a real treat when I find an off-the-beaten-path museum."

Skylar liked museums, too.

"I have a collection of antique signs," he said.

He did? Skylar fought the impulse to show her excitement. "Can I see them?"

His somber face told her he didn't wish to talk about this—or whatever thought they conjured. Skylar doubted the signs themselves made him upset. They must have reminded him of something.

"I'm sorry. Never mind." She welcomed the distraction of the menu and the waitress who took their drink and dinner order.

"I have a house in a gated community," he said.

Startled, Skyler looked at him. Why was he so vague about this? Gated community where?

"It's basically a ghost house. Linen covers the furniture and chandeliers. I bought it when I was with Renee. When I told her about it, she confessed she didn't want to have children."

Oh, so he had bought the house in anticipation of starting a family. With a woman named Renee. Skylar felt a pang of jealousy. And she was never jealous. He seemed to have acted too quickly, however, buying the house before telling Renee.

"Why haven't you sold it?" she asked.

"I decided to wait for the market to improve. I figured I might as well make some money on the deal."

That made sense and was smart.

"It's in a nice neighborhood where the houses back up to open space and are relatively far apart It's got privacy and great views."

Skylar wouldn't say she was impressed, but she was. Immensely. If ever she could live in a city, it would be in a place he had just described. Renee must have lost her mind to give up a man like him. Not wanting to have babies was a big issue, though. She couldn't imagine leaving him had been easy.

She imagined marrying him and having a baby. She had never thought this intently on that possibility with any other man. Oddly, the idea was titillating. She didn't know what to do about this alien feeling. Could it be that she hadn't considered having children before now because she hadn't met a man who made her want to? But why Julien? He would force her to choose between her ranch and him.

The ranch wasn't truly hers, though. Her parents owned it. Didn't she want something of her own?

Like an interior design business...

Skylar had spent the rest of dinner exchanging flirtatious looks with Julien, unable to shake the fantasy of getting pregnant with him. Now she walked beside him outside, him holding her hand and keeping her close. She'd noticed him searching their surroundings as he usually did, but he hadn't taken her hand as a safety precaution. No, she felt his own reaction to their evening together.

"We might have company," he said.

Jarred from her floaty feeling, she resisted the urge to look around.

"Maybe it's nothing, but let's see if we're being followed."

"How would anyone know where we are?" she asked. It was unnerving how her attacker could so easily find her.

"I didn't see anyone follow us here, but I suppose it's possible."

Someone very careful could have. Whoever they were up against had to be clever and experienced. Had Julien had been distracted by her? Was that why he hadn't seen?

She got into the BMW and Julien began driving, all the while keeping watch through the rearview mirror. He took a left and then a right, heading back onto the highway.

Skylar looked in the passenger-side mirror and saw a car turn onto the highway behind them.

"We're being followed," Julien said.

He sped up. The car tailing them was some kind of Chevy. Julien's BMW definitely had more horsepower. He slowed and made a U-turn. Next, he took out his pistol and rolled down the window.

Unsure if the other driver was armed, Skylar crouched low and watched Julien aim his gun as he passed by the other car. He never fired.

Skylar sat up and looked back. The other car didn't turn around and follow them.

Breathing a sigh of relief, she faced forward and leaned her head back. Had Julien intimidated the person, or had the car simply not been following them? She felt safe with him but she really needed this to be over.

Chapter 11

Julien could see the tail had spooked Skylar. Now
that they were back safely in his apartment, he decided to try to calm her nerves. And maybe a little
something else...

Choosing a good red from his wine refrigerator,
he poured the rich-scented liquid into two glasses.
Going to where she stood at the living room window, he offered her a glass. She flinched slightly
as though startled from some dark thoughts. Then
she smiled and her pretty eyes lifted to his as she
turned and took the wine.

He put his down on a side table and went to the
television, which had a nice sound system. Navigat-

ing to a music app, he found some country music and set it to play at a comfortable volume. Then he walked back to Skylar.

"What are you doing?" she asked tentatively.

"You seem like you need a break," he said.

"A romantic one?"

"Sure, if that's what you prefer."

Sipping her wine and keeping her increasingly flirtatious eyes on him, she said, "You like playing with fire, don't you." It wasn't a question.

The danger of wooing her was to his heart and to hers if this all came crashing to an end. He wasn't in the mood to think about that, though. What was wrong with having a sexual fling? They were both adults.

"Geography is becoming less and less important to me," he heard himself say.

She didn't respond right away but she must know what he meant.

"You would live on my ranch?"

"It's not your ranch." They'd best not forget the ranch belonged to her parents.

"It will be."

After her parents died, but then she'd have to split the asset with her siblings.

He stepped closer and took her hand, drawing her to him and slipping his arm around her, feeling the warmth of her lower back under his hand. "I'm tired of fighting this, Sky."

Her gaze went to his mouth and returned to his eyes, going all smoky. "No one but my mother has called me Sky in a long time."

"Oh yeah?" He began to sway with the music. "Who was the last one?"

"Bryce, the executive who worked for my father and tried to marry me for my money," she said. "It sounds a lot better coming from you."

That was encouraging. He took her hand in his as he continued to sway. "I think we should forget our differences and conduct some more testing."

"'Conduct some more testing'?" She breathed out a laugh. "You think we should have sex to test out how we jibe?" She slid her free hand up his chest, sending an electrical current zipping through him.

Keeping the subject in a lighthearted context helped to air what had been bothering him. He was now certain that Skylar had been suffering the same affliction. Fighting the urge to just go ahead and sleep together.

Was she really contemplating taking him up on this? He enjoyed looking into her amazing blue eyes awhile.

"I've been attracted to you from the first moment I saw you," he said.

She smiled at his direct admission. "It was the same for me."

"Well, that doesn't happen every day," he said.

"No, and that could get us into a lot of trouble."

"I would never hurt you." He didn't add *intentionally*.

"I would never hurt you, either."

"I will always be mindful of your feelings," he said.

"And I yours."

Wow, they had reached an agreement. Excitement made his pulse jump into faster beats. He pulled her to him so their hips met and kept moving to the slow country song. Her smile had faded and heat had darkened her eyes.

"What did we just decide to do?" she asked.

"Let's start with dancing," he said. "There is no schedule to go with this."

"Okay. That sounds safe." She rested her head on his shoulder.

He put his head beside hers. "I'll do everything in my power to make you feel safe." And he would. While a far off inner voice warned he would be the one who walked away feeling vulnerable and heart-broken. He ignored it and fell into the essence of Skylar and the way she made him feel right now.

Skylar danced with Julien for several minutes, feeling his warm breath on her neck, his muscular body moving with hers, his one hand holding hers, the one on her back making her tingle with anticipation. She worried what would happen if they forged ahead with blind passion.

She didn't have to deny herself sex with Julien. He did make her feel safe. He wouldn't make love with her knowing they'd never work out. He would do so *without* knowing whether they would work out. She would risk her heart, probably more than she ever had, but maybe Julien was worth that risk.

She lifted her head to look at him. His eyes were low-lidded and sultry, drugged by the desire they felt for each other. Right then she fell the rest of the way into committing to taking this to the next level.

Now unhindered, the floodgate of desire opened. She was free of the shackles, the fear that had held her back before.

Tipping her head a bit, she waited for him to accept her invitation. He did, slowly and with great care. His lips touched hers. They stopped dancing at the same time.

Skylar lost all awareness except of Julien and the way kissing him made her feel. They had done this before but there had always been that hesitancy that interfered. Now that she knew where this would lead, her entire body sizzled with delicious anticipation. She moved her hands up over his shoulders and slid her fingers into his hair.

Julien put his hands on her back and gradually deepened the kiss. Skylar reached a feverish state in seconds. As though sensing that, Julien withdrew and looked into her eyes. Then she saw he'd had the same reaction. She could see it in the set of his brow and the way he breathed. She could also feel his hardness. The need to have him inside her became almost unbearable, alarmingly so.

Julien moved back and took her hand. He walked toward the hall and she went with him into his bedroom, dimly lit by a lamp beside the king-size bed. He turned to face her and his eyes never left hers as he bent to remove his shoes.

That was a good place to start. She pushed off her shoes.

He took her hand again and tugged her to him. Her hands came against his chest and his arms went around her. Then he kissed her, soft and slow, much like before. He expertly wooed her, not rushing as their passion might have them do if he didn't keep it leashed.

When he lifted his head, his gaze drifted down the front of her. "I almost don't want to take that dress off you. You look so beautiful in it."

He warmed her with his words, especially since he sounded as though he meant every one. "All right, we can stay dressed," she teased.

Chuckling, his desire came out in a rich baritone. He stepped back and began unbuttoning his shirt.

Feeling like her bold self, Skylar reached behind her to unzip the dress. Then she slipped the garment off her shoulders and shimmied it down her legs until she stepped out of it.

He dropped his shirt as he looked his fill of her in a lacy bra and underwear. Still in his trousers, he walked to her. Her flesh broke out with goose bumps as his hand glided over her skin from her waist to her back.

She put her hands on his bare chest, momentarily distracted by sparks of heat before preventing him from pulling her to him.

"No fair," she said, taking the waistband of his pants in her hands and unfastening them. He pushed them down and kicked them aside.

"You're wearing more than me now."

"I don't have socks," she said with a slight smile.

He bent to remove his, sending them to the growing pile of discarded clothes.

Skylar couldn't stop herself from looking at the hard length of him straining against his underwear. The evidence of his desire hitched hers up a notch. He didn't move toward her, indicating he would wait for her. He wanted her ready.

She was.

Stepping toward him, she again put her hands on his chest, this time enjoying the soft skin over the shape of his fit muscles. His abdomen was ribbed. Sliding her hands to his rear and slipping her fingers inside the waistband of his underwear, she pushed them down.

Julien took his cue and reached for her bra. Unclasping the front, he freed her breasts. After looking at her for a nearly uncomfortable amount of time, he touched them, cupped them and then ran his thumbs over her nipples.

Skylar could ward off temptation no longer. She looked down and took his member in her hand. Its hard warmth quickened her breath and made her hotter.

She felt him abandon her breasts and push down her underwear. Both of them completely naked now, Julien again took his time taking her in visually. She watched his face, so reverent and impassioned.

At last, he put his hands on her hips and followed the curve of her waist back up to her breasts. He kissed her, his mouth moving with hers in loving gentleness. She moved her hands to his back as he pulled her against him.

The skin-to-skin contact inflamed her. She pressed her mouth firmer to his and he reciprocated. She knew he intended to take this slowly, but she couldn't wait any longer. Looping her arms around his shoulders, she kissed him even harder and pressed her hips against him.

Lifting her, Julien took her to the bed and slipped on a condom. He didn't take down the covers, just set her on top of the quilt. She opened her knees as he came to rest on top of her.

His mouth trailed over her neck and down to her

breasts, taking one and flicking his tongue across her stiff nipple, and then treating the other to the same exquisite ecstasy. He then moved on to her stomach, sending goose bumps spreading again. She sank her fingers into his hair as he kissed his way back up to her mouth.

"I need you inside me," she rasped against his mouth.

"I need to be inside you," he replied with equal passion. "I've never needed anything more."

His words washed over her, ignited her more. She felt the same.

Probing her, his entry was tortuously slow, sinking in deep and then withdrawing. The friction infused her entire body and mind with sensation. She raised her hips in a wordless entreaty for him to go deeper.

At last he seemed to lose control and thrust harder. Skylar lay her head back into the mattress, closing her eyes to sheer pleasure. He hit a spot that sent her soaring and he penetrated over and over, escalating the intensity until she burst with a cry.

He groaned as he came just after that. Then his movements gradually slowed until he was still. He collapsed on her, his head beside hers as they both regained normal breathing.

Skylar had known making love with Julien would be explosive but what she hadn't prepared herself for was the intense connection she felt. Her heart had fallen for him much harder than she'd anticipated. It was as though love had instantaneously entrapped her. The significance of what had transpired began to weigh heavy.

Neither one of them was ready for something this serious. Apart from their different lifestyles, Julien wanted a family, but he wasn't actively looking for a wife any more than she was looking for a husband. Besides, he still had issues with his last serious relationship. He had bought a house for them, only to be disappointed over how wrong he had been about the woman. Trust would not come easy for him, especially since Skylar had never contemplated having a family. She felt swept away on a tidal wave taking her far off course. She was headed in a direction she wasn't even sure she wanted.

She needed time away from Julien. She couldn't think straight with him nearby. As a woman who had always been certain of her decisions, she didn't recognize this new person that Julien seemed to be extracting. Was she growing in a healthy way or was she being dragged from a life she loved?

Julien woke before Skylar the next morning. She slept on her side, facing him, left hand on the pillow and long lashes touching her face in deep slumber. Feeling himself harden, he carefully got out of bed. Last night had rocked him in a way that had crumbled his foundation. How could a woman feel so wrong for him and yet so right at the same time?

He showered and dressed in jeans and a white Henley, memories of their lovemaking haunting him the whole time. In the kitchen he made coffee and heard Skylar running the shower. Soon he would have to face her, and he didn't think he could pretend he wasn't disturbed.

There was more than a good chance she would end up the same as Renee. Different circumstances, different women, but the same ending. He would not walk away from this unscathed. Skylar would be a woman he would never be able to forget.

He toasted some bagels and put out some salmon and cream cheese, then a bowl of strawberries, yogurt and granola. By the time he had the table ready, Skylar emerged in jeans and a flannel shirt. She appeared ready to go back to work.

She briefly glanced at him and poured coffee. At the table, she sat across from him.

"This looks good," she said.

"It was quick and easy," he said.

They sipped coffee and picked at their food. He read the news on his phone for something to do.

This was worse than he ever could have imagined. "Sky…"

"Don't." She held up her hand. "I can't talk about last night yet."

They needed to talk about it. He began to wonder if he should have another P.I. assigned to her case and then immediately shot the idea down. He wouldn't trust anyone with her safety.

"If I'd known it would be like that…" He what? Would he have stopped it? He couldn't have known and there'd been no stopping last night.

"Julien." She finally looked at him steadily. "I need to be away from you for a while."

He thought of the attacker out there somewhere, always watching. "No way."

She shook her head, closing her eyes and flattening her hand on the table. "Yes, Julien. I need time to think. My life is careening out of control and I need to get a grip on it. I can't do that with you always near, with us…"

With them craving each other like a couple of ravenous animals? He could not argue that.

"I'll be safe. I'll go to my parents' house. They're out of town for a couple of weeks on a trip to Europe. Corbin is staying there. I'll be all right. I just need a day or two."

Although he worried she would be all right, he could use a few days to himself, as well.

"You can stay at my house if you want to be close," she said.

That was something. "Will you call me so I know you're all right?"

"Sure."

Hearing her voice might be just as detrimental

to his state of mind as seeing her, but he needed to know she was safe.

"All right. I'll take you there."

"Take me home first. I'll drive my truck over."

"You won't leave on your own, will you?" he asked.

"No. I just need to be able to drive myself home when I'm ready."

Home, and back to him. She didn't know how long she would need and wanted to be able to leave on her own timetable. He related to the way she felt. What happened between them had changed their perception of their lives—or threatened to alter its course in a way they least expected.

Skylar used her key to get into her parents' house, locking the door behind her. She'd made sure she wasn't followed, as Julien had instructed. She texted him to let him know she'd made it, leaving her purse by the door and rolling her small luggage to the lower level guest room. She could hear the television in the family room. It was Saturday, so Corbin must be there.

She went to the family room and found him in a bathrobe, reclined on the couch with a remote in his hand. His hair was a mess and she was sure, if not for the housekeeper, this room would be cluttered with signs of his mood.

"You look like you haven't showered in days." Skylar went to a chair and sat.

Corbin looked at her, bleary-eyed and lethargic. "I've been working from home."

"I bet that's going well," she said.

"What are you doing here?"

"I'm going to stay a couple of days." She'd rather not discuss why.

"What's wrong with your house?" Corbin asked, sitting up and adjusting his robe. "I thought that investigator was staying with you until that shooter was caught."

"Well…" Oh, she might as well spill it. "He's the reason I'm here."

Corbin's eyes grew more alert, coming out of his self-induced stupor. "What did he do?"

"Nothing. We're getting too close, that's all."

"Ooooh." He wiggled his eyebrows. "So you finally found someone who can handle you and who isn't after the family fortune?"

"Something like that."

"If you like him, that's a good thing, isn't it?" he asked.

"I like him *too* much." Way, way too much. "Uncomfortably."

"I don't see the problem. Why run away?" He reached for a bag of chips and ate one.

"Why indeed." She sighed and held out her hand

for the bag, which he gave her. "He's a city man and I'm a country girl. What can I say?"

Corbin drank some of the soda on the coffee table. "Dad made you a country girl."

What was he saying? She couldn't believe it.

"Just like he made me an executive," he added.

"You love being an executive," she said. "You love money and power."

"Yeah, but ever since Ambrosia kicked me out, I've been wondering about my roots."

Was it a coincidence that she had been, too? Had they both encountered people who made them question their paths?

"Don't get me wrong, I'm not going to do something crazy like change my career, but what would I have done if Dad hadn't been such a stickler when we were growing up?" he said.

"Funny, I've been wondering the same thing—not what I would have done. I don't regret taking over the ranch operations, but this isn't my ranch. I didn't buy it."

"No, you were born into wealth," Corbin said sarcastically.

She studied him awhile. He was genuinely busted up over Ambrosia. "I've never seen you like this, bro. It's like you…grew a conscience overnight."

He looked insulted. "I have a conscience."

"Maybe it was buried by your penchant for blonde airheads."

Now he just looked sad. "I'm swearing off women for a while."

"Probably wise," she said, deciding not to give him too much of a hard time.

He reached for a chip and ate it. "I hired a couple of guys to help me move some furniture from the house the other day. When I got there, she was throwing a wild party. The place was trashed. We used to keep it so clean and organized. I didn't know she was so…untogether. We got into a fight in front of all her weird friends. I never knew she had friends like that. Come to think of it, we never did anything with anyone she knew."

"Exactly why you need someone genuine, Corbin."

"How do you find a woman like that?"

Skylar shrugged. "I suppose you have to be able to recognize one when you meet her."

Corbin sighed and ran his fingers through his disheveled hair. "Ambrosia tried to stop me from taking the furniture I wanted, but I took it anyway."

"No reason she should get everything," Skylar said.

Boy, the two of them were a wreck. For very different reasons, but they'd both been derailed by their relationships.

"What are you going to do?" she asked.

"I don't know. Hire a heartless attorney and keep Ambrosia from taking all I've got."

"Are you going to stay here in the meantime?"

"No. I rented an apartment. I have people setting it up for me."

Corbin liked to have people do things for him. He liked feeling important.

"What are you going to do?" Corbin asked.

Skylar took a few moments to consider that. "I don't know."

"What's keeping you from him?" Corbin asked. "It can't only be because he's a city guy."

No, it wasn't. And she was beginning to see that. "The way he makes me feel…it scares me."

He considered her awhile.

She had essentially told him she had strong feelings for Julien and this was much more than a casual thing.

"You're already in love with him," Corbin stated.

He hadn't asked her if she loved Julien. He'd said she *did* love him.

Oh, no. What if she did?

She couldn't possibly. How could anyone fall in love with someone in such a short period of time? She had heard of love at first sight, but really? That could happen to her?

No, she refused to believe that. She was in lust with him for sure, but love was something deeper.

That didn't mean she wouldn't fall in love with him. In fact, it would be easy to fall in love with him. What would she do then?

She had so much to work out in her mind, she didn't know where to begin.

"Don't sweat it, sis," Corbin said. "We can watch movies today and get drunk tonight. Tomorrow we can work on our personal issues."

Yes. Tomorrow. Not right now. She was a jumbled-up mess. Tomorrow she'd deal with it. She was glad to have her brother for support and glad she could be there for him. Some might call that denial, or escape. Not her. Because, no matter what she did, tomorrow would come and she would have to face the seemingly insurmountable emotions swirling inside her.

Chapter 12

Later the next day, Skylar reclined on a lounge chair next to the indoor pool. She had shared meals with Corbin and each of them did some healing. She had spoken with Julien last night and this morning. He had made her feel better by telling her they could take it slow, meaning they wouldn't be intimate again. While she appreciated his optimism, their potency didn't give her much confidence. She doubted she could keep her hands off him, much less his off her. She had, however, come to a conclusion.

Skylar hadn't asked for a whirlwind affair, and she could do nothing about the way she felt. She could accept that. She also could not predict the future. Whatever happened would happen. She was not ready to give up the life she had built on the ranch. Right now, today, she would not give it up. And she could not allow herself to give it up for a man. Any decision that major had to be for herself and no one else.

Sometimes her job of running the ranch seemed like her father's decision and not hers. Looking back, she didn't know if she had gone that route for herself or for him. At the time, the idea of running a cattle ranch had excited her. Working her way to the level of ranch manager had given her a great sense of accomplishment. She would never regret doing that. She had earned it. But she had to be honest with herself. She had chosen her college major for her father, not for herself. She was one hundred percent certain she would have gone to college for interior design had her father not pushed her in the direction he had.

At peace with everything, Skylar felt she could face Julien and deal with living with him until she was safe again. She would handle whatever became of them at that time. Not a weak person, she would get through heartbreak if it came to that. Meanwhile she would do whatever she could to minimize the damage, like taking it slow.

Feeling much better, she left the pool and went to put on a dress and pack up her things. It was time to go home. She hadn't brought much, so in a matter of minutes, she said goodbye to Corbin and sent Julien a text, telling him she was on her way.

In her truck, she drove down the long drive to the two-lane highway. She made a right and headed toward her house, the driveway not far down the road as her home was on the ranch property. Just a few seconds later, she saw a large SUV come up fast behind her. Julien's warning to watch out for a tail had her on high alert. But this vehicle didn't follow her. It kept coming, until it rammed into the back of her.

She shrieked in alarm and struggled to keep the truck in a straight line, swerving before she righted the vehicle. Her heart pounded and she felt her palms sweat, nearly slipping off the steering wheel. Taking a look in her rearview mirror, she didn't see the SUV. Until it appeared at her side. Skylar gasped as she saw a man in a mask driving. Before she could evade him, he jerked his vehicle to the right. The sound of grinding metal was deafening. Again, Skylar struggled to keep the truck on the road.

The SUV veered to the right once more and then crashed hard into her side again. Skylar was jostled in her seat, held in place only by her seat belt, and went off the side of the road. Before she could correct her path, she hit a tree head-on. The airbag exploded and that's the last thing she saw.

* * *

When she opened her eyes, she was in the back of an SUV. She sat up and discovered her ankles and wrists had been zip-tied. Her heart raced with fear.

Calm down.

Panicking would do her no good. The masked man was driving the SUV. His eyes shifted to the mirror and saw her.

"Who are you?" she asked, not expecting an answer. "Where are you taking me?"

Probably somewhere to kill her.

He didn't reply.

She glanced around and didn't recognize the road. How long had she been out? Several minutes, it would seem.

The driver turned onto a dirt road and, about fifteen minutes later, came to another one. This road was a driveway. There were a lot of trees here.

She searched around for something to use as a weapon. There was nothing in the back and nothing in the back seat. She could see a gun on the console next to the driver. That made her sick to her stomach. Was that how he would kill her?

Ahead, she could see a small cabin. It was in terrible disrepair and had likely been abandoned, or at least not visited in several years. The driver parked and got out, taking the gun with him.

Skylar's heart beat frantically and she began breathing fast.

Stay calm!

The man opened the back and aimed the gun at her while he used a big knife to cut the zip-tie at her ankles. "Get out," he spat, his voice raspy and low.

She did as he ordered.

With the gun digging into her back, he grabbed her arm and forced her toward the cabin.

"Why are you doing this?" she asked. "All I saw was you digging and that plastic bag lying on the ground." She had to assume this was the killer, as he had abducted her and now would murder her.

"Be quiet," he said.

She didn't recognize the voice. Was he disguising it? She tried to identify him. Physically, he was about the same size as Wes McKann, but she couldn't see his face.

At the door, he let go of her and turned the knob. She looked around. The clearing was too large. She would never make it to the cover of trees before he shot her.

He shoved her inside and kicked the door shut. There was no furniture in the cabin, no kitchen appliances, either. The wood floor was dirty.

"Sit down," he said.

Skylar went to the wall between the kitchen and living room and sat with her back against where the wall ended.

She looked up. The man had turned to look out a window, though he still had his gun aimed at her. What had him so distracted?

Not wasting any time, she kicked upward and knocked the gun out of his hand. It sailed through the air and fell to the living room floor. She scrambled to reach it first, but the man dove for it and rolled away.

Instead of shooting her, he went back to the window.

He glanced at her. "If you try anything like that again, I'll kill you."

Wasn't he going to kill her anyway?

He aimed his pistol through the window and fired. Then he went to the door and disappeared outside, firing some more.

What the...?

She heard answering gunfire and knew Julien had arrived. Relief flooded her body. She went to the window and saw that the masked man had climbed into the SUV.

Julien fired at him, breaking the passenger window. The masked man kept low as he turned the SUV around and raced down the dirt road.

"Skylar!" Julien shouted. He sounded desperate.

"In here!" she shouted back.

Seeing her in the window, he visibly sagged with relief. He charged into the dilapidated cabin and took her into his arms.

"Are you all right?"

"Yes." She leaned back as he took out a pocket-knife and cut the tie on her wrists. "How did you find me so fast?"

"He took your phone with him. I tracked you all the way here," he said.

"Thank God for your gadgets." She let her head fall to his chest, having started shaking with the easing of adrenaline.

"What happened?" he asked.

"He ran me off the road. I crashed into a tree and was knocked unconscious. He tied me up and put me in the back of his SUV and brought me here."

Julien began to check the place out. He searched every room and returned to the living room.

"There's nothing here," he said.

"He must have found this place and planned to get rid of me. Maybe he thought it would be a long time before anyone found my body." Skylar rubbed her wrists, which had turned red from the tight zip-tie.

Julien saw her and took her hands. "You aren't okay," he said.

"It's nothing. I'm fine." Thanks to him and his loyal vigilance.

He looked into her eyes and she saw his concern.

Pulling her to him, he held her close. "No more leaving me," he said.

She shook her head. "No more leaving you."

Keeping her hand, he walked with her to his BMW. After her two days of reflecting on their night together, Skylar felt much more confident about handling Julien. She had thought seeing him would send her back to that fearful, hesitant state of mind, but all she felt was good to be with him again.

Of course, that was probably because he had saved her. She'd see how she felt later, after a long, hot bath and a funny movie. And Julien right by her side.

Sheriff McKenzie met them at Skylar's house, Julien having made the call on their way back. She explained all that had transpired and described the man.

"He looked like Wes," she said.

"It wasn't him," the sheriff said, stunning her. Why would he say such a thing?

"Charlotte called earlier today and said she was staying with her parents," he said. "She didn't tell anyone because she didn't want Wes to know. I had the local authorities verify that it was Charlotte McKann I spoke with and they did."

That came as a startling blow. Skylar looked at Julien, who didn't appear as surprised as her.

"They've had some domestic issues for some time now and she's filing for divorce," Sheriff McKenzie continued. "There's been no physical or verbal abuse. From what I can gather, Charlotte is not happy being a cowgirl."

Skylar almost laughed at the way the sheriff said that. She didn't, though, because something rang true in her soul. She had grown up a cowgirl and had loved every minute. Still did. But was that her true calling? Oddly, she could relate to Charlotte. Maybe not completely. Charlotte had likely never had an affinity for ranch life but had married Wes anyway. Skylar could hardly blame her. Wes was an extremely masculine man, with good looks to attract just about any woman he chose—if they could get around his brooding tendencies. He truly did need a woman to break through that austere wall.

"I've closed her missing person case," the sheriff said, looking at Julien.

"Why didn't she want Wes to know where she was?" Skylar asked, still unwilling to dismiss Wes as a suspect.

Sheriff McKenzie shrugged. "She claimed he loved her and would do anything to hang on to her."

"She feared him?" Skylar asked.

"She's alive, Sky," Julien said.

Yes, and she understood that. She was just having a difficult time wrapping her mind around Wes's character. Okay, so he wasn't a murderer, but why had Charlotte run?

"Right," Sheriff McKenzie said. "He isn't a killer, but he isn't a man who gives up easily."

That painted Wes in a much more romantic light. He would fight for a woman he loved. Now he had lost that woman. Charlotte had disappeared from his life. Abandoned him. A man like Wes McCann wouldn't take that lightly. Charlotte feared him. Made him feel like a monster.

When he wasn't.

Skylar now realized that Wes was a misunderstood man. He kept to himself and lashed out when he perceived threats. Social threats. Personal threats. She suddenly felt contrite for not seeing that sooner. And yet, he reacted poorly to those perceived threats.

Skylar suspected Wes had a history that impacted his ability to socially interact and she wondered what it was. He may not realize the dysfunctional parts of his past, but he was not beyond redemption.

Be that as it may, she and Julien were at a roadblock in the investigation. Charlotte was alive and well. The last missing person was Benson's wife, Audrey.

Hearing Julien continue the conversation with the sheriff, Skylar returned to the present.

"With Charlotte safe, that leaves Davett the only other suspect," Julien said.

"Yes, and my office will be looking into him a lot closer. I'll keep you posted," Sheriff McKenzie said.

Julien nodded. "This changes my focus considerably." He turned to Skylar. "Is it possible that the masked man fits the physical description of Benson Davett?"

Skylar thought on that, mentally comparing build, height, size and other physical characteristics. She recalled seeing the masked man's dark hair and eyes. His eyes had also been dark. His voice had not been loud, but she could say it had been commanding. The timbre, however, was different.

"It's possible if Davett deliberately changed the tone of his voice." She looked at Julien and could immediately tell he had decided Davett was his number one suspect.

A few days later, Skylar got her wish to take Julien to a festival. He walked with her toward the food trucks lined up around a flurry of activity. A country music band played. A Ferris wheel turned and other rides had kids screaming. People walked with dogs, and children held cotton candy, sodas and stuffed animals. Skylar came for the fun and Julien came because he knew the lawyer would be there today. He knew because he had arranged to have his phone bugged, something he had done without police knowledge.

Skylar looked fetching in a blue spring dress with a light, flowy, waist-length jacket. She had her hair down and wore some light makeup. She didn't dress like this very often and he had a feeling he had something to do with it. He preferred to think that anyway.

"Do they have hayrides here?" he asked.

"Hayrides. Pony rides. Carnival rides. Everything."

"Let's start with the Ferris wheel, then maybe win you a stuffed animal, take in some food trucks and country music and finish up with a hayride."

"Now you're talking like a cowboy," she said.

"A city man who has been coerced into a hayride."

She laughed lightly. "You saved the best for last."

"Cities have festivals, too," he said.

"Yes, but not in *this* kind of setting." She reached her arms out and turned in a circle.

This festival was on the county fairgrounds. It smelled like horse manure and hay, and rolling hills surrounded the buildings and festival grounds.

She took his hand and all but dragged him to the Ferris wheel. They stood in line and shortly thereafter had their seats.

Julien enjoyed being with her. It didn't matter where. He hadn't told her, but he had needed that break as much as she had. Their lovemaking had rocked him far more than he had anticipated. Sure, he had known sex with her would be great, but he had not anticipated it'd be life-changing. Add to that the incredible fear that had gripped him with the thought of losing her to a madman, and a sense of panic and lack of control had hung over him ever since.

Although he never felt a stronger need to guard his heart, he didn't want Skylar to know. He didn't want to hurt her. He could not get past the fact that he had been severely burned before with Renee. He had told Skylar about her but he had not revealed the extent of the damage her betrayal had caused him. Yes, he considered it a betrayal.

Renee had led him to believe she'd felt the same as he had. She'd talked of a house in a rural subdivision, with two kids and a dog. Going on vacations. She had said she loved him, that she had never met a man who made her feel the way she did. Then she'd turned around and thrown it in his face. Everything she had said about having a family with him had been a lie. She had lied about loving him, too. After they broke up, Julien surmised it had been his trust fund that had attracted her to him. But when faced with what she'd have to do to get it, Renee had abandoned her gold-digging plan.

He really did not want to go through the pain of betrayal again.

"Well, that isn't how a Ferris wheel ride should go." Skylar's words jolted him from his reverie.

Julien looked up and realized he had been in troubled thought the entire ride, paying no attention to her. The wheel stopped and they exited the ride.

"Sorry."

"What were you thinking about?" she asked.

He wouldn't get into that now. Not today. "Come

on. Let's go win you a stuffed animal." He took her hand and walked with her to the Shoot Out the Star game.

"Of course, a gun game," Skylar said.

Though she sounded jovial, he could see she wondered what had had him so preoccupied.

At his turn, he picked up the BB gun and aimed for the tiny red star. He fired several times until the star was gone, then put the gun down and looked from Skylar to the booth attendant. She wore an openmouthed smile while the young man with long hair looked stunned.

"You Jessie James or somethin'?" the man asked.

"I was a cop."

"No fair, man."

Skylar chose the giant white tiger and on they went to the country music band and food trucks. There were tacos, hotdogs and hamburgers, three types of barbecue, ice cream, mac 'n' cheese, and one that offered Cuban sandwiches.

Skylar veered toward the Cuban and ordered a traditional roasted pork sandwich, as did Julien. They found a picnic table and listened to the music while they ate. All the while, he felt Skylar's curiosity, or maybe it was trepidation, as though she didn't have to be told what had transported Julien so far away from the present. She couldn't promise him his dream and he couldn't promise her a future.

Nevertheless, being with her made him feel good.

He looked around for Benson and spotted him sitting with his paralegal, Maria Morales. No one else from his firm was there and Julien found it peculiar that the lawyer would not only attend a food truck festival, but that he would come to a small town like this. Benson didn't strike him as a country guy. He also didn't seem to be thinking much of his missing wife. Rather, he seemed relaxed.

As Julien watched, Maria leaned closer and said something that made Benson smile. Maria was a stunning, dark-haired, dark-eyed woman who wore a low-dipping red blouse. The way the lawyer looked at her set off an alert inside Julien.

Were they having an affair?

As he and Skylar sat there listening to the music, Julien didn't take his eyes off the couple. After about thirty minutes, Benson and Maria headed for the parking area. Julien planned to look into their relationship further. For now...

"How about that hayride?" he said to Skylar.

She smiled and he knew that being with him made her feel good, too.

As they threw out their trash and headed for the horses and buggies, the mood began to lift. Julien was going to enjoy this. He had never been on a wagon before; this would be a first. He had never ridden a horse before that last time, either. Though he had grown up on a farm, it had been nothing like Skylar's ranch. There'd been no livestock. Still, being here brought back memories of his boyhood, none of which were bad. He began to wonder what had driven him to the city. The isolation, yes. Being far away from his friends, yes. Nothing fun to do...

Now that he'd thought about it, he realized those had all been the aspirations of a young man embarking on manhood. Isolation wasn't terrible. His friends had all gone their own ways and were now living their own lives. And as for fun things to do? He was having fun right now.

"You're doing it again," Skylar said.

He climbed up onto the back of the wagon and took a seat beside her on a bale of hay.

"Sorry," he said. "It won't happen again."

"It's all right. What's on your mind?"

He put his arm along the back of the wood rail behind her. "Let's not talk about that now."

She met his eyes in an intuitively understanding way. "I'm torn, too, Julien. No matter what, we'll both make the right choice."

Her time alone had given her closure, apparently. He wished he could say the same. The lesson the past had taught him was too painful to ignore, however. Judging from what Skylar had just said to him, she likely already knew that. He felt connected to her more than ever, and didn't see how he could ever give her up.

Chapter 13

Julien waited with Skylar in his BMW outside Benson's law firm. Rather than announce their arrival this afternoon, they'd question Benson's workers again—this time about his personal relationship with his paralegal. Scanning the parking lot, he recognized the lawyer's executive assistant from their earlier meeting. At the time, Harper Evans had had nothing to say, but he'd try again. Julien opened his door.

Skylar stopped him. "I'll stay here. I don't want her to feel intimidated. Having two people descend on her might make her clam up."

"All right." He got out and walked toward the woman.

A brunette in her early twenties, Harper stopped walking when she saw him. She held herself in a refined manner, but her eyes took on a wary look. That was enough to tell Julien she feared what he would ask.

"Hello, Ms. Evans," Julien greeted. "I'd like a word with you."

"You already had a word with me. What do you want now?" She turned a worried glance back at the office building.

"I'm still investigating the disappearance of Mr. Davett's wife, and I received a tip that he may be having an affair with his paralegal, Maria Morales. Can you comment on that?"

Harper began walking toward her car. "I can't help you any more than I already have."

Julien followed her. "Mr. Davett's wife could be dead, Ms. Evans." When she turned to him, he asked, "Is he really worth protecting?"

"No, but my job is." She looked nervously at the building again.

Something had her spooked. "You've heard about the investigation into Audrey's disappearance, haven't you?" Julien asked.

"Yes, of course. We all have. It didn't hit home

until you came asking questions. We thought she'd probably just left him."

"Why would you think that?"

Harper didn't answer right away. She took her lip between her teeth briefly.

"I saw him with Maria last night at a food truck festival in Walden. Just the two of them," she said.

She met his eyes for long seconds. "I've seen them together in the city, too. I was out with some friends and he was with her. He didn't see me and I left before he could. She goes into his office and closes the door a lot. I've heard them talking and it's too personal to be professional. They flirt, you know? I don't know if they're sleeping together but I'd be surprised if they weren't."

"How long have they been behaving that way?" he asked.

"I first noticed it about six months ago. But, thinking back, they could have been an item before that."

Audrey had gone missing around a month ago. Now Julien had just found a motive. Had Maria lied when she'd confirmed that Benson had been working late the night of his wife's disappearance? Had the paralegal simply provided her lover a convenient alibi? Or was she the one responsible for Audrey's disappearance?

"There's something else," the assistant said. "Benson suspected his wife was having an affair before he and Maria got together. I heard him arguing with Audrey on the phone about it."

Audrey was having an affair? Julien thought on that for a moment. Maybe she'd been going to divorce him and he hadn't wanted to lose half his assets to his cheating wife. Or did her new lover have something to do with her disappearance?

At exactly five o'clock, Julien and Skylar arrived at Audrey's lover's place of employment. They had tracked him down thanks to a neighbor and apparent close friend of Audrey's who had told them the man's name. Police hadn't questioned the friend yet and she hadn't offered any information because she didn't think Audrey's lover would have harmed her. She also didn't think Benson would, either. They had been a couple who lived in peace and quiet despite their unhappy marriage.

Harvey Lawrence was the CEO of a tech company in Dallas. He lived in the same neighborhood as Maria and Benson. His executive assistant had told them he could see them at the end of the day. Now he let them into Harvey's posh office on the top floor of a twelve-story building.

A tall man with a thick build, Harvey approached them with an outstretched hand. "My assistant says you're from a private investigation agency?"

"I am," Julien said, reaching to shake the man's hand. "Julien LaCroix. And this is Skylar Chelsey, a witness I'm protecting until we can solve Audrey Davett's missing person case."

"Ah. She needs protecting?" Harvey asked.

Skylar wasted no time speaking up. "I saw a man attempting to bury a body on the border of my property."

Harvey looked from her to Julien. "And you think the body might be Audrey's?"

"We hope not, but yes," Julien said.

Harvey motioned for them to take a seat. "What brings you by here?" he asked.

"We've learned you were having an affair with Audrey," Julien said.

"Yes, but we split up almost two months ago. I heard about Audrey going missing on the news, but I didn't feel I could help the police, so I didn't contact them."

Two months? That was before Audrey had gone missing, Skylar realized. She looked around the office and saw a photo on the console behind his desk. A blonde woman smiled with Harvey and their two teenage kids.

"Who ended the relationship?" Julien asked.

"I did. I decided to try to make my marriage work. If not for us, for our kids."

"How did Audrey respond to that?" Julien asked.

"She wasn't happy, but she respected my wishes. I felt bad, but we're both married. We knew what we were getting into from the moment it started.

We had been seeing each other for about six months before it ended."

Julien nodded.

"Does your wife know about your affair?" he asked.

"No, and I'd prefer she never does."

"Of course, but I will warn you that we may have to talk to her. Are you certain she doesn't know? Some people react differently when they discover their spouse is being unfaithful."

Harvey grinned cynically. "If you're suggesting my wife went on some kind of revenge killing, I can assure you, she is the opposite of that. She can't kill ants and she's afraid of everything. Heights. Deep water. Diseases."

Skylar noticed Julien didn't react to that.

"Besides," Harvey went on, "I've seen no change in her and she would have confronted me if she did know."

Julien nodded noncommittally. "I've got some other leads to follow, so that's it for now."

Skylar couldn't tell if the man was relieved or more worried with how calm Julien was. He stood and shook Julien and Skylar's hands.

"If you have any other questions, just let me know," Harvey said.

"Thanks." Julien ushered Skylar out of the office and down a hall to the elevator.

"He doesn't seem like the type to murder anyone," Skylar said as they rode in the elevator.

"I agree, but we'll keep him in a back pocket for now."

Outside, Skylar got in Julien's BMW and they headed back to his place, where they'd once again decided to hide out. A few minutes into the drive, Julien's cell rang. He checked the caller ID and answered. Skylar watched his face tense up as the seconds ticked on.

"I'm on my way. Stay in your room until I get there."

Instantly, Skylar knew it was Sawyer.

"Sawyer said his stepfather hit him," Julien said as he disconnected.

She supposed she had expected something like that to happen. Her heart rebelled against the injustice. No one at that age should have to live under those conditions.

Julien drove fast and, after about thirty minutes, they pulled up along the curb of the street.

The house was lit in two windows and the porch light was on. Skylar waited in the car. She would rather not get in the way of a domestic violence incident.

Maybe fifteen minutes later, out came Sawyer with Julien, who was carrying a suitcase. As the boy neared, Skylar saw his black eye. Instinct took over and she got out of the car and went to him.

"Are you all right?" she asked, touching his cheek and then inspecting the rest of him.

"Yes."

"Let's get him out of here." Julien opened the back door.

Sawyer got in and Skylar got in with him. "Are you hurt anywhere else?"

He looked embarrassed as he glanced at her. "I'm okay."

"What happened?" she asked.

"He started yelling at me, telling me to do stuff, like get him beers. I finally refused and told him to get his own. That's when he hit me."

"He wasn't in the house," Julien said. "I looked."

Skylar bet he'd looked. And if he had found him, John Larkin would have paid a price for harming an innocent kid.

"Where was your mother during all of this?"

"Drinking with him. She doesn't care what my stepdad does. I thought she did, but she doesn't. All she cares about is drinking."

"She was passed out on the couch," Julien said with a bite in his tone. "There were liquor bottles and beer cans all over the kitchen. I took pictures."

Sawyer would definitely be removed from that house now. Good. He deserved a better life.

"I'm sorry I lied," Sawyer said.

Julien looked in the rearview mirror. "Don't sweat that, kid. I knew you had your reasons."

"John said he'd kill my mom if I told anyone," he said. "He said he'd kill me, too. I believed him."

"He won't get anywhere near you now, Sawyer," Julien said. "I'll make sure of that. You're safe now."

Sawyer blinked slowly, looking tired but relieved. He relaxed against the seat.

Skylar looked at Julien's eyes in the rearview mirror and, for a split second, felt connected to him in a different way. A parental way. It was a warm and loving glow all through her insides. The rush caught her off guard and she averted her gaze to the window and the darkness passing by.

Back at Julien's apartment, she helped Sawyer get settled into the spare room. There were only two bedrooms. They were big, but this meant she would be sleeping with Julien. While that disturbed her, Sawyer was more important.

They had taken him to the hospital first. He had some other minor scratches and bruises—all were photographed—but other than his black eye, he was in good health. That was a relief. It was so hard witnessing the effects of abuse on a child, and she felt a tug on her heartstrings she'd never experienced before. She realized she would do anything to keep this boy safe. And that reaction surprised her, the intensity of it. She had never been aware that she possessed such a fierce maternal instinct.

Soon after seeing Sawyer off to bed, she saw he had already slipped into exhausted sleep. She smoothed his hair and turned out the light.

Julien was on the phone with the social worker when she stepped into the living room.

"What did Tracy say?" she asked when he ended the call.

He walked to her and took her hands in his. "With her help, I filled out foster care and adoption papers right after Sawyer went home. I knew this day would come. I knew something bad would happen and he would be catapulted back into the system. Tracy said Sawyer can stay here until the process is complete."

Skylar felt hugely confused. "Why didn't you tell me?"

"I wasn't sure if I could. I don't even know if I can call this dating." He let out a disgruntled breath. "I want—no, I *need* to protect that kid." He jabbed his finger toward the bedroom where Sawyer slept. "I don't know if I'll adopt him, but he'll be in my care until Child Services finds him a good and loving home."

Skylar could only stare at him. Her feelings about him, about children, family—her entire life—were a jumbled, messy ball of stupefaction.

"I didn't ask for this," Julien said. "I didn't plan for it. It just happened."

Like them. All of the events of the past several

weeks had crashed upon them—upon her. One day she had been carrying out her everyday routine and the next her life had exploded into a series of unpredictable happenings. She would never be the same again.

Chapter 14

Four weeks passed with no movement in the missing person case. Julien had kept surveillance on Benson, but he hadn't deviated from his normal routine. The shooter hadn't tried to attack again, either. Things had been quiet. Too quiet. Julien kept feeling that danger would jump out at them at any moment.

Skylar convinced him to go back to the ranch. Not only did she need to be there, she thought the environment would help Sawyer. Julien agreed only after arranging further security measures. He installed additional motion detectors farther from the house so there would be earlier warnings if anyone came onto the property.

Tonight, Skylar enjoyed making spaghetti. It had been a rainy day, chilly and breezy, and as the evening progressed, the weather had intensified. But inside, she felt cozy and warm. The aroma of the sauce simmering and the sound of a Disney movie completed the bliss.

Julien sat with his feet on the coffee table, Sawyer sat next to him. It was a wonder the boy had taken to him so quickly.

Sawyer looked up at her as though sensing her gaze. His contented eyes blinked with a soft smile. She felt her own answering smile along with a surge of affection.

He looked back at the television and she resumed her task of preparing dinner.

The three of them had fallen into a smooth routine. She and Julien took Sawyer to school and picked him up every day. She worked the ranch and hired a new deputy ranch manager, who was really good and could take over the operations when she wasn't there. Julien's manager had left. She could come and go as she pleased. She wasn't working the long days she had before Julien had come along, and she didn't miss it. Immersed in decorating his apartment, she found great joy in that.

She and Sawyer had gotten to know each other a lot better. Actually, she and Julien *both* had. Sawyer's appearance in her life felt like some sort of divine intervention. He liked animals and frequently drew them with the art supplies Skylar had bought him. He read science fiction and watched nature shows and family movies. Marvelous, how a boy from his background could have so many admirable aspirations.

Skylar had grown up privileged, never having to overcome the perils of poverty or the self-destructive cost of addictions. Her menaces had come from parents who sought money, affluence and assets.

"Okay. Dinner's ready." She set their plates on the table and sat at the end.

Julien turned off the television and he and Sawyer came to the table, taking seats to her left and right.

"I spoke with Tracy today," Julien said.

That must have been when she had worked with her deputy ranch manager this afternoon. "Oh?" She saw how Sawyer perked up with attentiveness.

Julien glanced at the boy with fatherly pride. "Sawyer's teachers reported he's improving in all his subjects."

Skylar sucked in a happy breath. "That's wonderful!"

Sawyer looked bashful with the attention.

As they finished their meal, the weight of what they were doing descended on her. They were acting like a family.

Were they a family?

No.

Not really. But Skylar felt she was playing a role, the role of a mother, and Julien the role of a father. The stable routine definitely helped Sawyer, but it couldn't last. Would they end up doing him more harm than good when Skylar's case ended?

She spent the next hour distracted by these thoughts. When Julien came back into the room after making sure the boy went to bed, she decided to broach what troubled her. "This is too much, Julien. He's getting too attached to this lifestyle and us."

"Well, we could get married and adopt him."

Though said in jest, that was a possibility. She knew Julien didn't want to part ways with Sawyer and the more time Skylar spent with him, neither did she.

Julien entered the Library with Skylar. The upscale bar, with bookshelves along one wall and muted lighting, suited Benson Davett's character. Julien and Skylar had followed him here. She wore a dark wig and a sexy red dress and he wore a cowboy hat and glasses with a suit.

Watching Benson meet up with two other men at a table, Julien sat with Skylar a few tables over.

"Looks like he comes here regularly," Skylar said when a waitress brought the lawyer a drink before he'd even ordered one.

"We'll talk to a few people after he leaves.

Meanwhile..." Julien opened a drink menu. "What'll it be?"

She chose a red wine and he ordered the same. Sawyer had the run of his apartment for the night. It was the first time they'd trusted him alone.

Skylar looked around. "I think my dad comes here."

"Yeah?"

"Always on business, of course."

She sounded cynical. "You don't like that about him?"

"I'm starting to resent him for being so... What's the word? Cal would say *elitist*."

He didn't press her. She seemed to be having an internal struggle over the path she had taken, most likely at the direction of her father. He hoped she'd follow one that led to them together.

As soon as the thought came, he felt himself recoil. His heart pulled him where his brain warned not to go, at least not prematurely.

"You look good in a cowboy hat," she said. He turned from Benson's motoring mouth with his two gentlemen companions. "Don't get too used to it." Although he joked, he actually liked wearing the hat.

"You like it and you know it." She smiled.

"Don't tell my friends."

She laughed. "You're also a natural on a horse."

He flirted back. "And you look good in city lights."

Their drinks arrived and he sipped as he admired her beauty. Her blue eyes mesmerized him. She must not dress up much but, damn, she sure looked great in that red dress.

A slow song began to play. Unable to ignore his heart, Julien stood and extended his hand to Skylar. When she looked up at him in question, he said, "We need to blend in."

She smiled in a way that clearly conveyed she was on to him, but she gave him her hand.

He took her to the dance floor, where a few other elegantly dressed couples moved. Holding her close, he swayed with her, one hand holding hers, the other low on her back. He twirled her slowly and gently, all the while reminding himself he had to keep his eyes on Benson, not her.

Halfway into the second song, he saw Benson raise his hand to a waitress, signaling he wanted his tab. Julien danced with Skylar a bit longer and then stopped and led her back to the table.

"What's the matter?" she asked. "Did it get too hot for you?"

Her teasing worked for their cover as an attractive couple having a romantic night out. He just had to tamp down on the heat she generated with those words.

He turned from watching Benson and saw her

sparkling eyes. "Be careful encouraging me." They might get to a point where it was too hot for both of them and then there would be no going back.

She sobered, no doubt catching his meaning.

He looked at Benson again, who paid his bill and spoke some parting words to his friends.

"Benson left. I want to talk to his friends," he said.

He flagged the waitress and paid their bill, noting that Skylar look around the bar, dubious and apprehensive. She had played her part well until now. Why? Had she realized how serious they were actually getting?

He couldn't think about that now. One of Benson's friends paid his tab and left. The other took his drink to the bar and sat, talking to the bartender as though they had known each other for years.

"Follow my lead." He held her hand and went to the bar.

He took the stool next to the man and Skylar sat to his left.

"I noticed you know Benson Davett," Julien said.

The man turned and observed him a few seconds.

"Julien LaCroix." He held out his hand. "I'm a P.I. working on his wife's missing person case."

"Ah." The man's face grew friendlier. "Arthur Moore. I'm an attorney. Benson and I went to law school together."

So he knew Benson well, or he must. "How's he holding up?"

Beside him, Skylar sipped the rest of her wine and decline the bartender's offer for another.

"As well as he can. He has his moments, I'm sure."

"He seemed to be fine tonight." As in, not troubled at all.

"It's been a while since Audrey went missing. What, like two months or something?" Arthur said.

"I'd be worried out of my mind if it was my wife." Julien glanced at Skylar, thinking he'd be that way if anything happened to her. "He doesn't seem concerned at all."

"I'm sure he is. Anyone would need an escape from that every now and then." As a friend of Benson's—and a long-term one—Arthur would naturally defend him.

"I received a tip that he's having an affair," Julien said.

"Who told you that?" Arthur's brow shot up.

"I never reveal my sources. How would you say his marriage was?"

"Fine. He didn't talk much about Audrey. They've been married a long time. So have I and, trust me, you get tired sometimes and need a break. That's what these nights are for. We get together two or three nights a week and talk about anything but our wives."

"He never mentioned an affair?" Julien asked.

"No. And if I was having an affair, neither would I," Arthur said. "Why are you asking me these questions? You don't think Benson had anything to do with Audrey's disappearance, do you?"

"I don't think anything yet. I'm doing my job and investigating all possibilities."

"Benson has a stellar reputation. He's well liked by everyone in the community."

"So was Ted Bundy," Julien said. Knowing they'd get nowhere with Arthur Moore, he stood. "Have a nice evening."

Skylar stood with him and together they walked out of the bar.

"What now?" she asked.

"We keep watching him." Julien stopped, spotting Benson still in his car and looking right at them. Did he recognize them?

The driver Julien had hired for the night pulled up and he let Skylar in first. From inside the sedan, he saw Benson on his cell phone. He didn't look at them again.

The next night, Skylar waited in the BMW with Julien outside Benson's law firm. It was seven and had to be getting close to the time Benson would leave. This stakeout business kept her mind off leading Julien into the bedroom. He had been a gentleman about that, having slept on the couch ever since Sawyer had arrived.

Thinking of Sawyer, the kid had proved himself trustworthy in the apartment by himself. He was still quiet and withdrawn, but at least he was doing well in school. He'd even made a new friend. Skylar had to admit that felt pretty darn rewarding. She had done something right with the boy. So had Julien. They had provided him a stable environment and they did things together, like watch movies, eat dinner and go to the ranch. Sawyer loved riding the horses.

Disturbingly, his mother hadn't tried to contact him at all. It appeared she had no intention of fighting the removal of her son from her home. Tracy had told them that John was still in the house, so it was for the best.

"It sure is better waiting with you than by myself," Julien said out of the blue.

"How many times have you done this kind of surveillance?" she asked.

"Many. It's part of the job. You learn a lot about people by watching them, seeing where they go, what their lifestyle is like."

She could imagine that. "Well, so far, Benson seems to live a decent life."

"So it appears."

"Is it common for murderers to seem normal?"

"More than you would like to think," he said. "Here he comes."

Skylar looked toward the building and saw Benson walking through the lit parking lot to his Mercedes.

Julien had the SUV running, but waited until Benson was about to leave the lot before commencing his tail. Benson didn't head for the bar tonight. Instead, he drove home.

When he took the exit to his house, Julien followed. "Let's fall back. He's going home and I know where that is." Julien slowed and let Benson's car go out of sight.

A few minutes later, they parked down the street from the lawyer's house.

"Nice." Skylar had expected Benson to live in an upscale neighborhood, and the massive two-story Colonial with pillars didn't disappoint. "It's going to be hard to spy on him in there."

"We'll see if he goes anywhere." He reached into the back seat and retrieved his laptop. "Besides, I had his house bugged."

"Along with his phone?" she asked.

"Yes." He tapped the keys on his laptop and brought up an earlier phone recording.

Skylar heard Benson's voice. "Hi," the recorded conversation began. "Are we still on for tonight?"

"Yes," a woman's voice answered. "I'm on my way now."

"Great. See you soon."

The brief call ended and Julien navigated to another program. Now Skylar could hear what must be happening inside Benson's house. He had turned on the television. She saw a light go on in one of the upstairs rooms and heard Benson moving around. It sounded as though he was changing his clothes.

Next, she heard him on the phone ordering Chinese. A white Audi pulled up into the driveway and out stepped Maria Morales, Benson's paralegal, in a short black dress.

She rang the bell and turned to look around. Skylar couldn't tell if her gaze lingered on the BMW. Then Benson answered, letting her inside.

"Late work night or something else?" Skylar wondered aloud.

"I ordered Chinese," she heard Benson say.

"Great." The sound of them kissing came through the speaker of the laptop, subtle but unmistakable.

"Something else obviously," Julien said. "Let's go get proof."

Skylar got out of the SUV and followed him through the shadows to the side of the house. Julien looked around. The houses were far apart and there were no outdoor lights here. She peered into the first darkened window. It was a home office with double French glass doors, through which she could see a dim living room. They went to the next window, this one lit. The plantation blinds were slightly open. Skylar spotted Benson handing Maria a glass of red wine. She looked at him with flirty eyes and he leaned in for a kiss.

Julien snapped photos with his cell phone.

Benson took Maria's glass of wine and put it on the coffee table next to his. Then he took her into his arms and kissed her with more purpose. He unzipped the back of her dress.

"Wait, is he going to…" Skylar sucked in a breath as the dress fell to the floor. "Oh, boy. I don't need to see this." But, like a bad movie, she couldn't look away. In minutes they were both naked.

Skylar felt sick and nervous, and awful about spying on such an intimate moment.

Julien finished taking pictures. "Okay, that should do it."

Skylar was all too glad to hurry back to the BMW.

Julien chuckled on the way. "For the record, I didn't enjoy that, either. But you should see your face," he said, chuckling some more. "You look green."

He eased her tension just like that. She smiled and got into the car. "How often do you have to do that?"

"Practically never. I don't take 'wives spying on husbands' cases."

Right. He prefers to take cold cases. Audrey Davett cases. "Well, I see a motive now."

"So do I," Julien said as he began to drive. "But is Benson responsible for Audrey's disappearance or is Maria?"

Last night, Skylar had felt like a detective as she'd sat beside Julien and his computer while he dug up all kinds of information on Maria Morales. She'd had a rough childhood, being raised in a trailer park by a single mom who'd had three DUIs. But Maria appeared to be normal on the surface. She went to college and developed an impressive résumé before going to work for Benson.

This morning they paid a visit to her previous employer, a criminal law attorney in Dallas.

Anthony Garrett ushered them to two seats facing his desk. He turned to Skylar. "Mr. LaCroix tells me he's protecting you from a shooter?"

"Yes. We think I may have seen Audrey Davett's killer attempt to bury her body," she said.

"I don't know any Audrey Davett," Anthony said.

"She's the wife of the attorney Maria Morales works for now. She's Benson Davett's paralegal," Julien said.

"Ah. Maria Morales." He nodded. "Which is the reason you're here. What can I do for you?"

"What can you tell us about her? What kind of worker was she and why did she leave?"

Anthony Garrett's brow lifted. "She was a hell of a good paralegal, but she had other issues. My partner came to me one day, said he'd had a brief affair with her and ended it after she began to try to drive him away from his wife."

Skylar glanced sharply at Julien, who stayed calm and focused.

"How did she do that?"

"She kept making demands. She called his house. She showed up on his doorstep. When he broke it off with her, she threatened to tell his wife."

"What happened?" Skylar asked.

"He told her if she did, he'd fire her. She left him alone after that, but I wrote her up with HR and gave her a warning. She seemed to take it pretty well and, for about a year, she was very professional. But then she started coming on to me."

Oh dear, the woman was a shark after her prey. She went after men.

"We were working late nights on a case together," the attorney said. "She started suggesting we grab working dinners, then she invited me to her place. I explained to her I was married, and happily so. She shocked me by saying that didn't matter. We could still have some fun together. Now, that might have worked for my partner, but I'm not that kind of man. I declined, of course. A few nights later, she came into my office and locked the door. She started to take off her clothes. I stopped her. She was humiliated and lashed out at me, calling me all sorts of names. I fired her on the spot."

Wow. Maria Morales was a bold, bold woman. Shameless, too.

"We think she may be doing the same with Benson Davett," Julien said.

"He's having an affair with her?" Anthony asked.

Julien nodded.

"And you think she may have done something to his wife?" he asked.

"Is she capable of that?" Julien returned.

"Murder?" Anthony's brow rose again. "Well, she did haunt me a bit after I fired her."

"Haunt you?"

"I caught her lurking outside my house, sitting in her car, just watching. I also saw her when I came to work in the morning. She called my office a few times—at least I believe it was her. She wouldn't say anything, just stay on the line for a few creepy moments until I hung up. After that, though, she left me alone and I never saw or heard from her again."

"Anything else you can tell us?" Julien asked.

"Isn't that enough? If you need me to answer the question you haven't asked, then, yes, I think she might be capable of murder."

Julien thanked him and they left the office.

"Maria may not have taken her stalking to the

next level, but I guarantee you she considered it," Julien said as they left the office building.

"You're convinced she's capable of murder, aren't you?" Skylar asked.

"Yes."

"What about Benson? Maybe he worked with her," she said.

"Maybe. Or maybe he doesn't know where his wife is or whether she's been murdered."

Skylar saw Julien search the parking lot, as he always did. Except this time, he seemed to have spotted something.

"Get behind this truck." He took hold of her and pushed her down behind the side of a pickup. A fraction of a second later, bullets pinged metal. Skylar shrieked, so unprepared for the sudden violence.

Julien drew his pistol and rose up to shoot. He fired three quick shots and then ducked for cover. More bullets clattered against the truck.

"Stay here." Julien rose and shot back again, then ran in a crouched position to another vehicle.

Skylar inched her way to the front of the truck and saw Julien shoot and make his way to another car, bringing him closer to whomever was firing at them.

He reloaded and straightened, running and shooting.

Skylar saw a dark SUV race from the parking lot.

Julien ran after it and then stopped to steady his

aim, firing several times. The rear window broke and a man ducked in the driver's seat.

Julien stopped chasing. Skylar walked out from behind the truck as he turned and jogged back to her.

"Are you all right?" He touched her arm.

"Yes." She was sure getting tired of being shot at, though. "How did that man know where we were?"

"He followed us."

Skylar was alarmed. "You knew?"

"I didn't want to scare you. He kept his distance and probably wanted to see where we were going. He won't follow us home, though. I will see to that."

Chapter 15

Sawyer's court proceedings were dragging on. During her last visit, Tracy had told Julien the Child Services proceedings could take about eighteen months. Meanwhile, Sawyer had already become a part of their budding family. Julien never voiced that to Skylar. He would only frighten her, or give her a reason to back off even more than she had over the last few days. He felt doomed to end up without her, and a fool for allowing himself to fall for her. He could fall madly in love with her. Hell, he probably already had.

Upon reflection, there was nothing he could have

done to prevent their initial attraction. That had had a life of its own.

This morning the apartment was quiet. Sawyer and Skylar were still in bed. Last night Skylar had expressed how much she missed the ranch, most especially her roan gelding, Bogie. They would head there this morning. No sense waiting around for Julien to hear if the sheriff had gotten search warrants for Benson's and Maria's homes. McKenzie hadn't promised anything since they had weak probable cause—a two-million-dollar life insurance policy, an affair with a woman who had attempted to snare other attorneys, and having an affair. Julien hoped it would be enough.

Hearing retching coming from his master bedroom, Julien stilled in the act of pouring a cup of fresh coffee.

Was Skylar ill?

He went to the room and knocked on the open door. "You okay?"

She retched again. He approached the bathroom and peeked inside. She was fully dressed and kneeling before the toilet. She hadn't seemed like she was coming down with a bug last night.

Another thought struck him and he stopped breathing for a few seconds. Could it be?

Skylar stood and ran some water, rinsing her mouth and then dabbing her face dry with a hand towel. Then, her head down, she braced her hands on the counter. At last, she lifted her head and met his gaze in the mirror.

He could see her alarm and also how she tried to subdue it, perhaps keep him from seeing how shaken she was. He was shaken, too, but he was also bursting with elation. The latter he fought hard to keep from showing.

"You all right?" he asked again, feigning ignorance.

She nodded. "I think so."

"Maybe you should lie down for a while. We can go to the ranch later today if you feel up to it."

"Okay. Maybe a pillow and the couch would be good." She straightened.

"I'll get you set up. Go ahead and get comfortable." He went into the master bedroom and retrieved a pillow. There were throws in the living room.

Skylar reclined on the couch with her hand on her tummy. She leaned up and he put the pillow behind her. She rested her head.

"Can I get you anything? A soda?" he asked.

"Maybe a ginger ale."

He poured some in a glass full of ice and put it on the coffee table. Then he sat in the chair near her and found something on television. Her eyes closed and he let her rest while attempting to get lost in a cooking show. But all that occupied his mind was Skylar, and the very real possibility she was pregnant.

About an hour later, Skylar sat up. She had sipped on her ginger ale until it was half gone.

Julien glanced at her and saw her wringing her hands. He let her mull through the shock of what he increasingly knew they'd have to face.

At last she straightened and looked at him. He warily met her eyes.

"I feel better," she said, matter of fact.

He resisted the smile her resilient tone tempted.

"I didn't think we were at risk," she said.

"I should have asked you about birth control," he said.

She lowered and shook her head in denial. "I can't believe this."

"Neither can I." But he couldn't say he was disappointed.

"It's one thing to fantasize about it, but it's totally different when it's for real."

She had fantasized about him getting her pregnant? "Yeah. I'd have to agree with you there."

That brought her head up. "You're amused?"

"No." He cleared his throat. "I'm as surprised as you. I wouldn't have seen this coming if a meteor struck with a message attached." It arrowed straight through their main issue, what kept them from really opening up to a serious relationship. They wanted different things out of life. He wanted to move to a suburban neighborhood and be part of a family he and the woman he loved created together. She had strong ties to her family ranch and had never contemplated having a family.

He was sticking his heart out into the unknown, risking pain he ordinarily would not with any woman, not after Renee.

"Meteor." She grunted a cynical laugh. "That's what it feels like."

"How about we start with a pregnancy test?" Before they worked themselves up in a tension-ridden frenzy, they needed facts.

"Right. Test."

Julien heard Sawyer in the shower. As soon as he was ready, they'd head out for the ranch. First stop: pharmacy.

Skylar alternated between flashes of utter panic to attempts at imagining what it would be like to have a baby. She already had Sawyer, and if she and Julien made it as a couple, she'd have a premade family even before she gave birth to another member.

She had to give Julien a large amount of credit. While she had been in the throes of reality slapping her face, he had remained as calm as a sea turtle. He had allowed her time and quiet to process the insurmountable realization that she was, in all likelihood, pregnant.

He even went into the pharmacy for her. Now they had arrived at her house and she went into the bathroom and took the test. But she couldn't look at the results. Instead, she brought the test stick out into the hallway, where she found Julien waiting like an expectant father. Sawyer must be in front of the television, since she heard a family movie playing.

He took the stick from her with a questioning look.

"I couldn't look," she said.

He held her gaze for several long, poignant seconds before looking down. Then he met her eyes again. "It's positive."

Skylar let out a hard breath and cursed mildly. She ran her fingers through her hair, her mind going a trillion miles per hour with endless scenarios and the torture of what lay ahead for her—for them.

"I need Bogie." She walked to the door.

"Not alone, Sky," Julien said.

She stopped and faced him. "I need to be alone."

"Okay, but at least let me ride behind you. I'll give you plenty of space and I won't talk."

She nodded once and left the house. She saddled Bogie while one of the grooms helped Julien saddle Willow.

Riding out of the stable, she headed toward her favorite route, along the fence line. She heard Julien behind her and his horse's hooves, along with a snort every now and then. His presence prevented Skylar from escaping into her own thoughts. She needed to sort out her situation, to come up with a plan. How would she deal with this? She couldn't begin to assemble any coherency.

Bogie bobbed his head and glanced back at her with a nicker.

"Yeah, I know." She patted his head. So in tune with her, he sensed her unsettled state.

The horse went into a trot and then a gallop without her urging. She loved running with him. She let him have free rein.

Remembering Julien wasn't an experienced equestrian, she looked behind her. He rode well for a beginner. Was there anything he wasn't good at? She grew annoyed. And he was nice, too. He patiently let her go through her stages of emotion and did whatever he had to do to see this new development through, including riding a horse like he'd been riding for years.

Arriving at the place where she had seen the man digging the hole, she slowed Bogie to a halt and stared at the spot. If it hadn't been for the gunman, her life would still be on track, her days on the ranch would be as usual.

Or would they?

She still would have met Julien. Rather than him with her 24/7, maybe they would have dated like normal people. The same chemistry would have sparked, though. She doubted any of what had transpired between them could have been avoided.

After several minutes stewing over her predicament, Skylar finally came to accept what nature had handed her. She was pregnant. She would have a baby. And Julien was the father, a man who set her on fire with unfathomable passion. That couldn't be all bad, could it?

She looked back and saw him about fifty feet away, sitting on Willow, watching her.

Turning Bogie, she rode to the side of him and his horse. He met her eyes in that way of his, confident and strong, ready for anything.

"What are we going to do?" she asked.

"Nothing for now," he said, sounding as though he had an answer for everything.

She wished she could be so sure. "What are we going to do nine months from now?"

He didn't respond right away. "Things will be different nine months from now."

"How so?"

"You and I will know each other better, for one. And, most likely, we will have arrived at a plan for our future."

Their future? As in…together?

"Don't worry so much. I'll respect your wishes, no matter what they are," he said and then reined his horse in a turn back to the ranch.

Did he mean he would live on the ranch with

her? Split time between them with the child? What about Sawyer? The more time she spent with the teenager, the less she wanted to part ways with him.

The questions echoed in her mind as she rode beside Julien.

He had to have some tumultuous thoughts about this. He was just being stoic to help her. And damn if that didn't attract her to him all the more.

Sheriff McKenzie called with news that the search warrant had been approved. On their way to Benson Davett's house, Julien couldn't stop the thoughts and worries from bombarding him. It had taken all his willpower to stay calm and supportive for Skylar. He wished he could do more for her. He wished they were farther along in their relationship. He wished he could make her see that having a family was not only the most natural thing in the world, it could also be the best thing that ever happened to her.

Julien knew this would be the best thing that ever happened to him. Even if he had to live with a dysfunctional arrangement like joint custody, he would have a child of his own.

Not to discredit Sawyer's place in all this. Another child in the mix would actually help the boy. He would be part of a family, a stable, healthy family—if Skylar came around and allowed them into her life.

He was glad when they arrived at Benson's residence; he could finally focus his mind on something other than Skylar and the baby. Sheriff McKenzie, who met them at the door, gave them the go-ahead to enter. The house was immaculate, not a thing out of place aside from upturned items as the search continued. Law-enforcement personnel were everywhere.

"So far, nothing is turning up," the sheriff said.

That was discouraging. Julien went to the back sliding-glass door. No one had started to search outside yet. He opened the door and stepped outside while Skylar remained inside talking with the sheriff.

Julien carefully walked the border of the yard, passing artfully curving flowerbeds that were springing to life. He checked for areas where someone may have dug and saw none. After he made his way to the other side of the yard, he came to the shed and found it secured with a master lock.

He looked toward the house and saw Sheriff McKenzie Skylar standing just outside the sliding-glass door.

"We found some keys in here." The sheriff went inside and a moment later reappeared. He brought Julien the keys.

Julien tried a few before one of them released the lock. He opened the shed and went inside.

"Here." Sheriff McKenzie handed him gloves.

"I'll get the team. Just look. Don't disturb or touch anything."

Julien began searching the shed, careful to do as the sheriff said. There were the usual gardening items—including two different kinds of soil shovels, one caked with dried dirt. That struck him as a potential piece of evidence. A photographer appeared and Julien pointed to the shovel.

"We need samples of that dirt," he told the sheriff.

When the rest of the crime scene investigators appeared, he left the shed and walked the rest of the yard. Nothing seemed out of place.

"Julien?"

He turned to see Skylar standing at the rear of the shed. He joined her there and noted that the ground different than the surrounding, mounded and chunkier and most important—void of plants.

"Sheriff," Julien called.

The sheriff came to them and as soon as he saw the ground, he hollered for the crime scene team.

Julien stood back with the sheriff and Skylar waiting while the forensics experts dug the ground, slowly and meticulously.

"We found something," one of the experts said.

Skylar clutched Julien's arm apprehensively.

"It's a body."

Skylar's hand tightened on his.

"Maybe you should go inside," Julien said.

"No. I'm all right," she said.

Julien stepped closer, Skylar going with him. The forensics team cleared dirt from around a partially decomposed body, buried behind the shed at a decent depth, plastic parted to expose the corpse. Julien could tell this was Audrey Davett based on his memory of her photo and what remained of the features of her face. They'd do a DNA test to confirm it, but this had to be her.

"No jewelry," one of the forensic team members said.

So, Benson had removed her jewelry before burying her?

The forensics team began bagging up several dirt samples.

"We also obtained a saliva swab from Benson. There was a hair sample taken from the trash bag we recovered from the dig site near the Chelsey property," the sheriff said.

Julien supposed he hadn't told them that before because they'd had nothing to compare the hair to until now.

"There's a box of trash bags in the garage, bought from a big-box store. Forensics said they could compare them to see if they came from the same source as the garbage bag that was buried."

"Wow. That's a big break," Julien said.

"It is now that we're here and we have been able to get DNA from Davett," the sheriff said. "Oh, and we also found emails between Audrey and an attorney. Benson must not have known about her second email account. The email she used for personal communications was cleaned out. We'll try to recover what we can, even though everything was deleted."

"Good work, Sheriff. Are you sure you don't want to come to work for Dark Alley?" Julien said.

The sheriff chuckled. "I'm just glad we'll be able to solve this case." He started to move away. "This is going to take a while. Why don't you and Skylar come with me to the station? We're going to bring Benson and Maria in for questioning."

Julien wouldn't miss that for the world.

Skylar waited with Julien in the room with a one-way mirror. No one was in the interview room.

Sheriff McKenzie entered. "Benson is refusing to talk. He cried lawyer."

Of course he did. He was a lawyer himself. He knew not to talk to detectives without an attorney present.

"Maria Morales has agreed to talk, however. We offered her leniency if she had anything to do with Audrey's murder. She may have known about it or even helped Benson in some way."

Two officers brought Maria into the interview room. She appeared nervous, eyes flitting from one cop to the other. After she was seated, one of them left and only a single officer remained. He sat across from Maria.

"I'm Detective Ross," the officer said.

Maria nodded.

"Why don't we begin with when you and Benson began having an affair?" Ross said.

"A year ago," she said.

"And how long had you been working for him at that point?"

Maria had to take a few seconds to think. "Five months."

She moved quick, Skylar thought, zeroing in on her man and going after him.

"How much did you know about his wife?" the detective asked.

"What do you mean?"

"Did you know anything about her? What she did, who she saw, where she went?"

Maria shook her head. "I knew Benson didn't love her anymore. He told me she was having an affair."

"When did he tell you that?"

"I don't remember. Maybe three or four months ago."

"Did he ever say he would divorce her?"

"No. He said she would take all his money and that he regretted not having a prenup in place."

"So, he had no plans to divorce or leave her?"

"Not that I'm aware."

"How did that make you feel?"

Maria didn't answer right away. "Well, naturally, I would have preferred he not be married, but with him wanting a divorce, I thought we would eventually be together."

"You must have realized he wasn't going to divorce her," Ross said.

Maria tapped her fingers on the table, clearly agitated. "Yes."

"And how did that make you feel?"

Maria tapped her fingers again. "Well, obviously, I didn't like it, but I knew what I was getting into when I got involved with him."

Skylar could see the detective was trying to get her to reveal emotion that might suggest motive.

"How much didn't you like it?" Ross asked.

Skylar smiled a little. Ross was a cool cookie, soft and mushy in appearance but cunning and hard in reality.

"I didn't like it, okay."

"Did it make you angry? Jealous?"

"He didn't love her."

"Didn't?"

Maria sighed hard. "What are you asking?"

"A simple question. Were you jealous?"

"No. Audrey didn't work. She met Benson when he was young. She isn't a career woman like me. She isn't smart. She's a homemaker."

She sounded so defensive that Skylar wondered

if she had been the mastermind behind Audrey's murder.

"What's wrong with being a homemaker?" Ross asked.

He hadn't even gotten to the hard questions and already Maria was unraveling.

"Nothing, but...Benson needs more than that, you know."

"Did he tell you that?"

"No." She grunted her frustration. "I—I just know him."

"Okay." Ross held up a hand, indicating he would back off on that line of questioning. "Did he kill his wife?"

She hesitated.

"Did he?" Ross asked.

"Yes."

Ross said nothing and the long silence put Maria on task to continue.

"We talked a lot about the problem of Audrey," she said. "You know, how it would cost him too much money to divorce her. I tried to convince him he would be all right even if she took him to the cleaners. He's a good lawyer with a successful practice. But he had his eye on the maximum bottom line, you know?"

Ross nodded.

"About a week before, Benson started saying he'd like Audrey to go away. He kept saying that, and asking me if I would like that. I told him I'd like for him to divorce her, but he always refuted that."

"Then what?"

Maria tapped her fingers on the table again, bending her head.

"Need I remind you that you could be facing serious criminal charges if you don't cooperate?" Ross said.

After a few seconds, Maria raised her eyes and held the detective's gaze. Skylar felt a chill with the coldness she saw in them.

"She's not telling the truth," Skylar said loud enough for only Julien to hear, despite the fact that the room was soundproof. "Not all of it."

"Yeah, that's what I think, too."

Skylar caught Sheriff McKenzie's sober glance before facing the one-way glass again.

Finally, Maria straightened regally and said, "He called one night…the night Audrey was reported missing. He wanted my help. He asked me to come to his house. He never invited me there. When I arrived, he said he'd secured our future and I had to invest in it. He asked if I wanted to be with him. I said I did. He then took me to the backyard and showed me the hole behind the shed. Audrey's body was in it."

Maria put the back of her wrist to her mouth.

"What an actress," Skylar said.

"He told me to start shoveling," Maria said. "He

told me if I didn't, it meant I wasn't serious about us being together. I was scared. I did what he asked because I didn't know what he would do if I didn't."

Now Maria's hand trembled as she wiped a tear from below her left eye.

"Oh, spare me." Skylar sighed her disgust.

"Mr. Davett should reconsider talking to us," Sheriff McKenzie said. "He's in another room, waiting for his lawyer." He went for the door. "I'll be back."

Detective Ross picked through some papers he had in a folder before him. "You worked for Anthony Garrett, correct?"

Maria drew her head back as though surprised that name had come up. "Yes."

"He fired you?"

"Yes, but—"

Ross cut her off. "He claims you stalked him. Pursued him for romantic interests."

Scoffing with a dismissive wave of her hand, Maria said, "He was threatened by me."

"Threatened?"

"I'm good at what I do."

"But you aren't a lawyer. You're a paralegal."

With another sigh, Maria averted her head.

Clearly the woman was delusional.

"Isn't it true you pursued these lawyers to better your life?" Ross asked.

"Who doesn't want to better their life? What's wrong with that?" Maria snapped.

"The men you pursued were all married."

"Unhappily."

Ross closed his file and stood.

"Where are you going?" Maria asked. "Can I go home now?"

"Not yet," Ross said, leaving the room.

The door opened where Skylar and Julien stood and the sheriff summoned them to follow. Skylar walked ahead of Julien to another room that looked into another interrogation room.

In there, Detective Ross took a seat across from Benson, who scowled with a low brow.

"My lawyer isn't here yet," Benson said.

"We thought you'd like to know what your mistress is saying," Ross said. "Maria said you talked a lot about Audrey. She called her a *problem* and told us how you said it would cost you too much money to divorce her." The detective paused.

Benson's mouth had tightened into a displeasured frown.

"She said she tried to convince you to go through with a divorce, but you had your eye on the maximum bottom line. Most significant is that she accused you of threatening her if she didn't help you dispose of the body. You showed her the hole behind the shed in your backyard. Audrey's body was in it."

"That is not true!" Benson roared. "She's the one who killed Audrey, not me."

"She did?"

"I want my lawyer. Maria is lying."

"You're going to prison for a long time if we can prove you murdered your wife, and right now we have plenty of evidence to place you under arrest. We also found evidence in Maria's apartment to arrest her. She also kept emails between the two of you that clearly show you were having sexual relations."

"Those emails were all part of her plan to entrap me," Benson said, then slapped his hand to the table. "Damn it, I said I want my lawyer!"

"You might be able to make things a lot easier on yourself if you tell us what happened," Ross said.

A knock on the door signified Benson's lawyer had arrived. It was none other than Anthony Garrett. Maria would flip out when she discovered that. Skylar figured Benson knew about her past with Garrett. But Maria's stalking had never been reported and there was no evidence proving it.

Ross gave Benson time to speak with his attorney. About an hour later, he was back in the interrogation room.

"All right. Let's begin with the first question. Did you kill your wife?"

The lawyer nodded to Benson.

"No."

"Where were you the day your wife went missing?"

"At work."

Workers at his office had confirmed that, Skylar knew, but he could have left anytime after he and Maria were alone. Maria's confirmation that he was at work until after seven could no longer be trusted.

"What happened after you arrived home that night?" Ross asked.

Garrett again gave a nod when his client turned to him.

"Audrey wasn't there. I tried contacting her, but she didn't answer her cell phone. When she didn't arrive home by ten, I called the police."

"Did you bury your wife in your backyard?"

"No!" Benson raised his voice. "I'm not a murderer and I would never kill my wife."

"Were you planning on divorcing her?"

"I was considering it."

"Why did you have a two-million-dollar life insurance policy on her?"

"We both have two-million-dollar life insurance policies. It was a decision we made together."

An officer entered the room carrying a small envelope and whispered something in the detective's ear. Ross took the envelope and glanced sharply at the man. When he left, Ross faced Benson and his attorney.

"I was told your wife's cell phone and a pistol were recovered from Maria's apartment. It appears she hid them in the floorboard of her bedroom closet."

Skylar sucked in a breath and grabbed Julien's arm. "She did kill Audrey."

"All it will take is some ballistics testing," Julien said. "Audrey was shot in the head."

"There were also bulky clothes and a black mask in her closet," Ross said, letting a ring fall out of the envelope onto his palm. "And this." He showed it to Benson.

"That's Audrey's wedding ring." Benson breathed heavier and ran his hand over his face. "She killed her. Maria killed her." He began to tear up.

Skylar's mind whirred. Maria was pretty tall. She could pass as a man if she dressed in bulky clothes. In Skylar's recollection, the person she saw digging could have been around Maria's height. So could her attacker. With all the action and the clothes covering her body, she could have passed for a man.

"Did you know Maria may have killed your wife?" Ross asked the very question that ran through Skylar's mind.

Benson wiped under his eyes and composed himself, looking to his attorney, who took a few moments before he said, "Go ahead and answer that."

"I did suspect something. She was at my house when I got home from work the day after Audrey went missing. She said she wanted to surprise me. I thought it was odd. And I noticed she was wearing dark jeans and a dark jacket with boots. She never dressed like that. I didn't think anything further of it. I asked her to leave since I didn't know where my wife was. She left."

"Were you aware that Maria told the police you were working late with her the day your wife disappeared?" Ross asked.

"No. Maria left early afternoon that day. I worked alone in my office until I left."

Skylar pieced together the time line she was hearing. Maria must have abducted Audrey after she'd left the mall and then taken her somewhere to kill her. Then the next morning, she'd driven to what she'd thought was a remote area—where Skylar had seen her digging. She'd replaced Audrey's body with a bag of trash. When the burial site didn't work, she buried the poor woman in Benson's backyard, hoping, no doubt, to implicate him.

"Was Maria at work the day after Audrey vanished?" Ross asked.

"She came in late. I didn't see her until about four."

So, what had she done? Skylar wondered. Had she driven Audrey's body around in her trunk until she's figured out what to do with her? If she had been abducted the previous day, where had Maria taken her?

"We'll make sure that abandoned cabin is searched," Julien said, as if reading her mind.

"Do they have enough to arrest her?" Skylar asked him.

"I'd say so. Audrey's cell phone? Her wedding ring? A gun and the clothes you saw her in? Yes. They've taken her car to search for evidence."

This had all taken a turn Skylar never would have guessed. Maria had been clever in her disguise. But not clever enough.

Chapter 16

Traces of blood were found both in the trunk of Maria's car and in the abandoned cabin. One of the neighbors reported seeing Maria's car turn onto the driveway, which is likely why she hadn't buried the body there. The blood in the car matched Audrey's and ballistics tied the pistol they'd found in Maria's home to the shell casings located near the spot where she had been digging. Maria Morales had been arrested for murder and any suspicions of Benson's involvement had been put to rest.

Skylar was safe now. Julien packed his things and would take Sawyer back to his apartment. He would give Skylar some time to sort through her feelings about him and about being pregnant. He hadn't told her yet. Sawyer was still in the spare room getting his things together.

Julien carried his duffel bag into the living room, seeing Skylar finishing up in the kitchen after breakfast.

She stilled in the act of wiping down a counter when she saw his bag. "You're leaving?"

Did she not want him to? "I don't think being presumptuous is good right now." And part of him was reluctant to expose himself to her too much. Renee's treachery still haunted him and as much as he felt for Skylar, he couldn't bring himself to trust her.

Sawyer appeared with his bag. "Aren't you coming with us?"

Skylar looked from Julien to the boy. "Not right now, Sawyer. You go on ahead with Julien."

"When are you going to be there?" Sawyer asked.

Skylar went to him and put her hands on his arms. "I don't know. Don't worry. You'll be all right."

"But we're a family. You both gave me a family. We can't split up."

"It will be all right."

"You and Julien belong together," he said.

"I don't know about that. We haven't known each other very long."

"I can tell you belong together. You love each other."

"I—" She glanced back at Julien.

"Okay. I get it." Sawyer walked to Julien. "Come on. Let's go. You two will come to your senses soon enough." He looked back at Skylar. "You know where to find us when you're ready."

When she was ready. She met Julien's masked expression. More like when he was ready. Maybe they both weren't ready.

"I'll be in the car." Sawyer left the house, obviously giving them time alone.

"That kid is too smart," Skylar said.

"Yes."

And maybe he was also right. Skylar walked to Julien and stood before him.

"Look, I know you're reluctant to trust anyone after Renee," she said. "But I want you to know that I would never commit to anything I wasn't one hundred percent sure of."

"Are you one hundred percent sure of having a baby?" he asked. "My baby?"

She had to let out a cynical breath. "Of course not."

He smiled slightly. "What about me?"

She had to be brutally honest. "Not one hundred percent, no. Maybe eight-five or ninety." She smiled at him to smooth the blow, if it came with one.

"Thank you for being honest."

She rose up on her toes, putting her hands on his chest, and kissed him. What began as a featherlight touch heated into a full taste of him. But she curbed her desire for more and stepped back.

"Let's take a few days to think things through," she said.

"All right."

"Call me whenever you want," she said.

"You, too." He took her hand and gave it a squeeze.

Their parting was as difficult as she'd imagined. Her heart felt like a brick of lead and her stomach turned—and not from morning sickness. She watched him go, and had to ward off the apprehension that she would never see him again. Because she knew one thing: Julien was further than she was from accepting what they had together.

It was nice not to feel as though she had to look over her shoulder. Skylar kept herself busy on the ranch. The work kept her mind off Julien for the most part. He was always on her mind, but the pain didn't really hit until nighttime, when she ate dinner alone and slept in her lonely, quiet house. How had she lived like this for so long?

She drank her tea and tried to get into the book she was reading on her Kindle. She finally gave up and let her thoughts take over. Leaning her head back on the living room chair, she stared at the ceiling.

Her mother had begun to get suspicious over how often Skylar went up to the big house. She didn't complain. She loved seeing her daughter so much, but she could tell something was wrong.

"What happened to Julien?" she had asked last night.

"He went home. We weren't really seeing each other."

"Oh, you can't fool me, Skylar. Your father and I can see there is something going on between you."

"Well, not anymore. I haven't heard from him in days. He obviously isn't as interested as I thought."

"He's just afraid. All men are. Your father was like that when we first met. He was scared I'd distract him from his true passion." Her mother had laughed.

Skylar would not compare Julien to her father. And she hadn't imagined their physical passion. Even Julien couldn't deny that.

Checking the time, she picked up her phone and called Julien's apartment. Today was Sawyer's birthday. She'd waited until now because Sawyer had said he'd had plans with a friend all day, but he should be home by now.

She called Sawyer's phone and he answered.

"Hello, birthday boy," she said.

"Hey, Sky. Thanks for the bike. I love it!"

"You are very welcome."

"You should be here. Julien bought me a cake and ordered pizza."

"Yum. I wish I was."

"It's not too late. Just come over. We can watch a movie."

Skylar would love nothing more. "It's not the right time, Sawyer. Please try to understand."

"I understand Jules is being stupid," he said.

Yeah, well, there was nothing she could do about that. "He has to work through his issues on his own. I can't help him with that."

"What issue does he have?"

Skylar sighed. How much should she tell this clever kid? "Girl trouble. He needs to get over someone."

"Who?"

"You'll have to ask him." She didn't feel right about being the one to air his past agonies. "Is he there with you?"

"Yes. You want to talk to him?"

Did she ever. But should she? She missed him so much. She missed his voice. His eyes. His heroism. What if she tried? Maybe if they started talking, that would give him the right nudge.

"Yes," she said.

She listened to Sawyer say, "She wants to talk to you."

After a few seconds, Julien said, "Hello, Skylar."

She closed her eyes to the sound of his voice. Then forced herself to remain strong. "Hello, Julien. When did Sawyer start calling you Jules?"

"A few days ago. The bike is nice. Sawyer rode it when he got home."

"Must be a pain taking it down from your floor."

"It's not so bad."

Silence fell over the line.

"How are you?" he asked.

"Fine. Working a lot on the ranch."

"Of course."

"How about you?"

"Fine. I'm between assignments."

Another silence fell over the line. *I miss you* almost came tumbling out of her mouth.

"Well," she said instead, "I should get going."

"Yeah. Me, too."

"Take care," she said, hearing how husky her voice sounded.

"Goodbye, Skylar."

After she disconnected, she dropped the phone onto the coffee table and put her head in her hands, struggling to keep tears at bay.

Julien put his phone down and leaned against the counter with his head bent, her words—*take care*— running through his head over and over, the sound of her voice echoing in his ears. He heard her emotion and it sparked a wave of his own. He had thought of nothing else other than Skylar and their baby. It didn't help that Sawyer kept teasing him with reminders about her.

"I miss Skylar's French bread pizza, don't you?" he had asked once.

He did.

"Skylar would have told you to be careful with that," he had said another time when he'd held a big chef knife at the ready to slice a tomato.

She would have. Skylar had a funny, sarcastic way about her. A sassy mouth. A sexy mouth. He missed that, too.

"When are you going to face it and admit you love her?" Sawyer asked.

Julien looked up and saw the boy had joined him at the kitchen island.

"She wanted to talk to you," Sawyer said. "That means she misses you."

"You're only fifteen. You aren't supposed to be that insightful," he said, straightening.

"I had to learn fast."

Unfortunately, he had.

"Who are you having girl trouble with?" Sawyer asked.

He had never felt this way before, so skittish and jittery. He missed Skylar like crazy and hearing her voice had only made it worse. A thousand arrows pierced his heart.

"She's someone I used to know," he said.

"Skylar said you need to get over her."

"Did she now?"

"You're afraid to be with Skylar."

"Okay, that's enough." Julien couldn't take it anymore.

"What's so special about that other woman anyway?" Sawyer asked. "I mean, compared to Skylar, is she really that great?"

That got Julien thinking. "No." No, Renee didn't compare to Skylar at all. It was what Renee had done to him that made him push Skylar away. But, really, did he want to keep Skylar away from him? Why was he so afraid? Because Sawyer was right, he was afraid. And that was so unlike him. Granted, he did worry about him and Skylar not working out. But was he actually going to let that stop him from trying?

"You're being stupid," Sawyer said.

Julien looked at him. "Yeah. I know that now. Thanks, kid."

"You can't go to her empty-handed. She'll probably be mad at you for a while."

"Yeah. You're probably right about that, too. Any suggestions?"

Sawyer thought a moment and then said, "Yeah. I have an idea."

Working her usual routine, Skylar was finished for the day but didn't feel like going home just yet.

She rode along the fence line, not because she had to, but because she couldn't escape her mind and heart. It was happening. Her heart was breaking. Her relationship with Julien had caused it. Exactly what she'd feared the most and tried the hardest to prevent had descended upon her. She couldn't fight it any longer.

Looking around at the Chelsey property, she realized none of it mattered compared to him. She would give up the ranch for him. For their child. The ranch wasn't hers. It belonged to her parents. She'd eventually inherit her share, but it was never her dream. She had never followed her dream. It wasn't too late to start.

She would probably have never come to this realization had she not met Julien. He'd changed her, made her grow. Had she changed him? Had she made him grow?

Returning to the stable, she handed Bogie over to a groom and then went to her deputy ranch manager.

She spotted him just outside the stable, getting ready to enter the corral. "Mr. Garrison?"

"Skylar. Hello."

"I need a word with you."

"Okay." He led the horse inside the corral and tied him to a post before facing her.

"You have been doing an excellent job here," she said.

"Thank you. Always good to hear."

"All of the workers and the animals seem to like you. I like you."

He didn't say anything but he could tell she was about to broach something important.

"How do you feel about taking over as the lead manager?"

"I'd be thrilled. Did something happen?"

"I'm thinking about taking a break or maybe just working part-time."

"Ah. Well, to be honest, I was looking for more than a deputy role."

"Why don't you come by my office tomorrow at ten and we'll finalize everything."

"Sure will. Thanks." He tipped his hat at her and she left the stable area.

Seeing the time was after six, she drove home. As her house came into sight, she saw Julien's BMW parked in the front but no sign of him.

She entered and both heard and smelled something cooking.

In the kitchen, she found him at the stove, searing some beef. Through the doorway, she saw that the dining room table was set.

"I had a key," he said.

She remembered giving him one. "What are you doing here?"

"Making dinner." He brought over a wineglass. "Ginger ale."

She took it with a smile. "Thanks."

"Sawyer and I had a man-to-man talk and he made me realize some things," Julien said.

"Where is Sawyer?"

"He's at my apartment. He shoved me out the door."

"What things did his wise young soul make you realize?" she asked.

"That I've been a major fool, for one."

"Major, huh?"

"Yes."

She sipped and felt a twinkle make its way into her eyes. He made her feel so good. And his eyes held a twinkle, too. She was so glad he was there.

"Your timing is perfect. I've got almost everything ready."

Skylar took her glass with her into the dining room. Julien had prepared a green salad and scalloped potatoes. She stilled when she saw a ring box on one of the plates.

Putting down her glass, she turned to see him standing behind her.

"Yes, that's for you," he said.

She picked up the box and opened the top. A big round diamond flanked by two sapphires sparkled. It was beautiful.

"Julien…" She didn't know what to say.

He took her hand and brought her around to face him. Taking the box, he removed the ring and slid it on her finger.

"I'm not asking because you're pregnant," he said, "I'm asking because I love you."

Tears of happiness stung her eyes.

"Will you marry me?" he asked.

She nodded. "Yes!" Then she threw her arms around him.

He lifted her off the floor and kissed her. As always with them, the impassioned heat spread through her. She wrapped her legs around him.

Free to love him without fear of being left in the cold, she kissed him back with fervor she had not experienced before.

"I'm not hungry," she said against his mouth. "I only want you right now. I thought I had lost you."

"Dinner can wait." He carried her up the stairs to her bedroom, putting her down on the mattress.

She put her hands on his face and kept kissing him as he unbuttoned his shirt.

"I was going to tell you this over dinner," he said as he threw his shirt aside. "I'll live anywhere you want. Here on the ranch. Anywhere."

She kissed him. "I just offered my deputy the lead manager role."

He returned her kisses, giving her room to remove her flannel shirt.

"Are you sure?" He stood to remove his jeans.

"Yes. I'm not sure if I want to live in a house you bought for another woman, but I at least want to see it."

"I didn't buy it for her. I bought it with kids in mind."

She shimmied out of her jeans and underwear and he unclasped her bra.

"Well, lucky for us we already have one on the way." She laughed lightly.

"Are you happy about that?" He kissed her. "That was something else I wanted to bring up over dinner."

She laughed again, slipping her hands in his underwear and pushing them down. "I was shocked at first, I have to admit. But the fact that it's yours changes everything." She met his smoldering eyes. "Yes. I'm happy."

He grinned his satisfaction. "You haven't said you love me yet."

"I love you. Now make love to me."

He pressed a hard kiss to her mouth and spread her legs with his. "Yes, ma'am." Without hesitation, he sank into her, going in deep and then withdrawing.

She was instantly transported to another world where only the two of them existed. He moved slow, drawing out the sweet tension. He met her eyes as he moved.

Their joining felt so much more powerful than the first time—if that were even possible—and Skylar knew the reason was that they had nothing to fear anymore.

Epilogue

Typical of her mother, Francesca had planned a whopper of an engagement party a month later. She'd invited all their friends and neighbors. So far, no one knew Skylar was pregnant. She wasn't sure when she wanted that news out. This was all so new to her. Never in a million years would she have anticipated her life would take such a drastic turn. But it did feel right. For the first time ever, she had no doubts whatsoever. Marrying Julien and starting a family was all she wanted or needed. Embarking into interior design would be secondary but something she looked forward to trying.

Skylar saw her brother come into the rec room

where people mingled at the bar and played pool. A woman appeared from behind him. Tall, with flowing black hair and a stunning though heavily made-up face, she walked like a model. Skylar reserved judgment until she talked with the woman.

Corbin saw her and walked over. "Engaged, huh?" He leaned in for a kiss on her cheek.

"Yeah. Who would have thought?" She glanced at Julien, who smiled proudly.

"Amber, this is my sister, Skylar, and her fiancé, Julien."

"Hello," Amber said in a singsong voice.

Skylar shook her hand. "How did the two of you meet?"

"At the Rusty Lantern," Corbin said. "I bought her a drink and we hit it off."

"What do you do?" Skylar asked the woman.

"I don't have to work," she said loftily.

"Lucky you. How did you manage that?"

"I married well when I was eighteen. Unfortunately, we grew apart as we got older."

Was she saying she married for money at the young age of eighteen? Skylar met her brother's look. He seemed headed toward the same mistake. She would talk to him later.

Just then she spotted Wes McKann enter the room. "I don't believe it."

Julien followed her gaze.

Wes saw them and approached.

Corbin left them to head for the bar with his new girlfriend.

"Wes, how nice of you to come," Skylar said.

Wes shook Julien's hand. "I figured I needed to make an appearance to smooth over my behavior of late."

"We're just happy to know your wife is all right," Skylar said. "I'm sorry I thought you killed her. Convinced, actually." She smiled in a way that might soften the words.

Wes let out a laugh. "That's the thing I like about you most. You say it straight and true." He sobered. "I wanted to tell you I'm sorry for the way I treated you both. I wasn't expecting Charlotte to leave me and I struggled a little with that." His somber face said he still wasn't over her. "Anyway. Congratulations."

"Thank you."

A woman approached that Skylar didn't recognize. She went straight for Julien and hugged him.

"Hey, Jules. Congratulations."

"Hi, Indie. This is Skylar."

"So you're the lucky lady. There have been a lot before you who've tried to snare him. You must be someone very special." She was a striking blonde with blue eyes.

"This is Indiana Deboe. She's a private investigator at DAI," Julien said.

Skylar didn't feel so curious anymore that this

beautiful woman knew Julien so well. "Hello. This is Wes McKann, he owns the ranch next to ours."

"Ah." Indie looked at Wes, her gaze lingering. "Nice to meet you."

"Likewise." Wes's response sounded stiff and a little unapproachable.

Skylar saw Corbin looking at Indie with more than casual interest.

"Can I get the two of you something to drink?" Skylar asked.

"I can get my own," Indie said, looking back toward the bar. She saw Corbin and her gaze stayed connected with his awhile before she headed over in that direction.

Wes left to talk to a man who had just arrived, leaving Skylar and Julien alone a few minutes.

"This is turning into an interesting party," Julien said.

"Very."

Romance was in the air. She hooked her arm with Julien's. She had hers right here.

He met her eyes and smiled before kissing her softly.

* * * * *

#2107 COLTON 911: AGENT BY HER SIDE
Colton 911: Grand Rapids
by Deborah Fletcher Mello
FBI agent Cooper Winston is determined to take down a
deadly pyramid scheme and PI Kiely Colton has the information
to make that happen. She's not going to let him push her out
of the search, but when danger flares, they're forced to rely on
each other and face the attraction they both fear.

#2108 COLTON STORM WARNING
The Coltons of Kansas • by Justine Davis
The last thing security expert Ty Colton wants is to play
bodyguard for a spoiled heiress. But just as he begins to
discover that there's more to Ashley Hart than meets the
eye, the threats against her are acted on—and the very
weather itself tries to tear them apart.

#2109 FAMILY IN THE CROSSHAIRS
Sons of Stillwater • by Jane Godman
Dr. Leon Sinclair is trying to rebuild his life when Dr. Flora Monroe
arrives in town and threatens his job...and his peace of mind.
But Flora and her twins are in danger and Leon must face the
demons of his past in order to keep them safe.

#2110 GUARDING HIS MIDNIGHT WITNESS
Honor Bound • by Anna J. Stewart
The last time he lost a witness, Detective Jack McTavish
nearly lost his job. Now, protecting Greta Renault, an artist
who witnessed a murder, is his top priority. As he's forced to
choose between believing her and saving his career, Jack's
decision could make the difference between life and death.

"Don't! I saw him. He was here." Her mind raced. Her
ankles wobbled in the ridiculous shoes Yvette had
convinced her to wear. Swearing, she reached down and
slipped them off, leaving them on the sidewalk as she
sped down the street toward the historic section of the
building. He couldn't have gotten very far. He could even
be back inside. Maybe he'd gone up instead of down.
Maybe… He had to be here somewhere. She spun in
circles. She wasn't imagining things. She had seen him.
He'd seen her. And there… She froze. Her breath went
cold in her chest. She stared across the street to beneath
the blinking pedestrian-crossing light.

"Greta." Jack's hands reached out for her.

She tore herself away. Falling, flailing. Horns blared.